The Waiting Sands

Susan Howatch was twenty-nine when she completed *Penmarric*, the bestselling epic saga of a Cornish family; it took her five years to write. Born in Leatherhead, Surrey in 1940, she was an only child and her father was killed in the Second World War. After leaving Sutton High School she took a degree in law at London University, but after working for a year as an articled clerk she was bored with practical law and decided to devote herself to writing. In 1964 she went to America and within a year her first novel was accepted for publication. While working on *Penmarric* she wrote five other novels apart from *The Waiting Sands* – *The Dark Shore, The Shrouded Walls, April's Grave, Call in the Night* and *The Devil on Lammas Night*; all of these, *Cashelmara* and *The Rich are Different*, are available in Pan Books.

Susan Howatch now lives in Ireland.

Also by Susan Howatch in Pan Books

Susan Howatch
The Waiting Sands

Pan Books London and Sydney

All the characters in this book are fictitious and are not intended
to represent any actual persons living or dead.

First published in Great Britain 1972 by
Hamish Hamilton Ltd
This edition published 1973 by Pan Books Ltd,
Cavaye Place, London SW10 9PG
8th printing 1980
© Susan Howatch 1966
ISBN 0 330 23598 2
Printed and bound in Great Britain by
Hazell Watson & Viney Ltd, Aylesbury, Bucks

There were still times when Rachel thought of Daniel. She would think of him at the height of summer when the city sweltered beneath the hazy summer skies to bring back memories of another land where the sun was cool and the sea breathed white mist over remote shores. She would think of him sometimes at night when she awoke for no reason and sat up listening to the restless city around her, the city so many thousand miles from the past she had no wish to remember. She would think of him when the other girls in the apartment talked of love and romance and happy endings, and she would say to herself how strange it was that she should think of him so often when she knew for certain now that she had never loved him.

She had not always lived in New York, but now she had been there nearly five years. Her home was in England, in Surrey, not far from London; she was the only child of an elderly Anglican parson and his wife, and for the first twenty-two years of her life she had moved in the orderly, old-fashioned circles of the world of the country vicarage. She had gone to a local day school, progressed from there to secretarial college where she had acquired the necessary skills without undue difficulty and then had gone abroad to Geneva for six months. On her return, she had begun to earn her living in London.

It had all been typical, a career duplicated by a great many other girls. She had several good friends, was happy at home, enjoyed tennis at weekends during the summer and in general was perfectly content with her life; certainly if anyone had ever suggested to her then that she would alter her entire circumstances radically by emigrating to a foreign country she would have been astonished and then indignant that anyone could suggest such a thing.

The only extraordinary and unusual element in her otherwise normal existence was her relationship with her friend Rohan Quist.

It seemed to her often that Rohan had been the most consistent thread in her life, his presence flickering across the pattern of the years like quicksilver darting over shifting sands. For Rohan had always been there. He had shared her past and she had shared his. She could remember clinging to the stays of her play-pen while he had ridden his tricycle up and down the drive to show off to her that he was free and mobile while she was still behind the bars of infancy. But later he had taught her to ride the tricycle, led her hand in hand to kindergarten, drawn her into all the intricate games of childhood, the societies, the sworn oaths, the pacts which led to adventure. 'And nobody's to say Rachel's too young,' he had shouted to his adherents in the pack he led. 'Because she's my friend!' She could see him now, eight years old, thin and wiry with thick straw-coloured hair and enormous blazing grey eyes.

Rachel's my friend . . .

And Rohan was good to his friends. Long afterwards when they were grown up it was he who would provide an escort whenever she wanted to go out, he who had the little red Volkswagen to take her on weekend drives into the country, he who had invited her to the May Ball at Cambridge where she had met a whole host of eligible young men. 'We'll say we're cousins,' he had ordered authoritatively. 'Then no one will get the idea that I have any possessive rights over you.' And no one had. She had danced the night away and drunk a little too much Heidsieck '59, and after breakfast at dawn in Grantchester when she was quite exhausted, Rohan had materialized from a punt on the river and had ferried her safely back to town.

There had been quarrels, of course, times when they were not on speaking terms. Rohan was an emotional extrovert who preferred to give vent to his grievances in a splendid display of rhetoric, and Rachel, who had more of an Anglo-Saxon temperament, found such exhibitions annoying. But the moods passed; the words were forgotten, and soon they were picking up the threads of their friendship as if nothing had happened and life continued as usual.

But they were getting older, and Rohan's grievances in a certain direction were becoming more acute.

'It's all very well,' he had said crossly, 'but I'm always the one who makes the effort, I'm the one who takes you around and introduces you to all the good-looking men. What do you ever do for me? When have you ever introduced me to a pretty girl? When? Just answer me that!'

'That's not fair!' Rachel had retorted, rising to an argument with spirit. 'What about all my schoolfriends? I constantly introduced them to you!'

'Hardly my type, were they? I mean, seriously—'

'Helen's very pretty!'

'But poor Helen,' Rohan had said in the tired voice he used when he wanted to annoy her. 'Absolutely no sex-appeal.'

'How the hell am I to know how you define the term sex-appeal?'

'No swearing, please. I always hate to hear women swear.'

'You're impossible!' Rachel had blazed. 'Quite impossible!' But she had felt guilty all the same. And then, when she had gone abroad to study French for six months she had met Decima in Geneva, and Decima was very different from the kind of girls Rachel had known at school.

When the six months had come to an end, Rachel and Decima had returned to England together and Rachel had introduced her new friend to Rohan at the earliest opportunity. Decima was staying with Rachel for a few days before returning to her home in Scotland; the three of them had planned an exciting weekend together before her departure. 'We'll have a grand time,' Rohan had said, jaw stuck out to show his aggressive determination to enjoy life to the full. 'My cousin Charles is coming down from Oxford and we'll make up a foursome. You remember Charles, the professor in medieval history, don't you, Rachel? He would do very nicely for you – you're always saying how much you like older men . . . Yes, that would be a good foursome. You and Charles, Decima and me . . .'

Decima and Charles had married less than four months later. After the engagement was announced, all Rohan had said was: 'It's just as well. She wasn't really my type – much more suitable for Charles, and I'm sure they'll be very happy . . . I

7

wonder if they'll live at Oxford all the year round? Charles used to spend the university vacations in Edinburgh.'

And Rachel had said: 'Maybe they'll stay at Ruthven.'

Ruthven . . . Rachel had never been there, but Decima had talked so often of her home that Rachel had evolved a clear picture in her mind of the house to which no road led, its grey walls imprisoned between the mountains and the sea, the savage coast of Western Scotland, remote, vast and unmarked by time. She had thought on more than one occasion how nice it would be to visit Decima there.

But Decima and Charles had been married well over two years before an invitation came, and long before then Rachel had resigned herself to the fact that she would never be invited since Decima had not bothered to keep in touch with her and their correspondence had soon lapsed. Rohan thought nothing of inviting himself to Ruthven now and then for a few days of fishing and shooting with his cousin Charles, and couldn't understand why Rachel did not merely arrive on Decima's doorstep, but Rachel was proud; if Decima wanted to see her, then Decima should write and ask her to come; until then Rachel had no intention of turning up where she was apparently not wanted.

Then finally after two years the invitation arrived out of the blue, and the chance came for Rachel to visit Ruthven at last. It was late summer; Rachel had just come back from a holiday in Florence and happened to be between jobs, so the invitation could hardly have come at a better time.

The postmark was Kyle of Lochalsh, the handwriting unquestionably Decima's. Rachel ripped open the envelope with a pleasant feeling of anticipation and eagerly began to read the letter inside, but a second later bewilderment had displaced her eagerness, and presently even the bewilderment had vanished, leaving her feeling both uneasy and disturbed.

'Dearest Raye,' Decima had written, 'I'm so terribly sorry I've been such a hopeless correspondent, and please don't think that just because I've not written much I never think of you. I have thought of you so much, especially when it's seemed that there's no one I can turn to, and I'm writing to ask if you can possibly come up to Ruthven for a few days. My twenty-first birthday falls next Sunday, and it would be such a relief if you could stay until after the celebration dinner party which Charles is giving for me on Saturday night. Please come, Raye. I may be behaving very stupidly by panicking like this, but I would feel so much less frightened if I knew you were beside me at Ruthven till after midnight on Saturday. I can't say any more than this now as I'm just about to leave for Kyle of Lochalsh to meet Rohan, but please, please come as soon as possible. I'll explain everything when I see you and meanwhile much love,

'Decima'

PART ONE: RUTHVEN

CHAPTER ONE

I

Shortly before the long-awaited invitation was sent, or even thought of, Decima Mannering was sitting on the window-seat of her bedroom overlooking the ocean and thinking of her friend Rachel. Rohan Quist was due to arrive that day at Ruthven to begin two weeks' holiday, and Decima always thought of Rachel whenever Rohan was due. The two seemed to be inseparable in her mind; it was as if they were husband and wife, she thought, or, to describe the relationship more accurately, brother and sister. It was odd how an unrelated man and woman could know one another since infancy and yet never become sexually involved with each other. It was not even as if it were a casual childhood friendship long since outgrown. They were nearly always together, almost inseparable, and yet it was quite evident there was no sexual attachment of any kind uniting them. It was really most curious. But then, remembering Rachel, one might perhaps conclude that the situation was only to be expected. Rachel had such an unfortunate attitude where men were concerned; she either frightened them right away or else she de-sexed any possible relationship by being apparently cold and withdrawn. There was some basic inferiority complex, of course; she had to be constantly reassured that a man was interested in her, and the need for reassurance led her to set up impossibly high standards which any admirer could not conceivably hope to attain. Or maybe there was no inferiority complex and Rachel was simply old-fashioned, desiring her various beaux to be pure knights in shining armour riding to court her on spotless white chargers.

Poor Rachel . . .

She could remember when she had first met Rachel in Geneva. Rachel had worn a very English tweed suit which was a little too big for her, and still wore her dark hair in braids coiled around the top of her head. Quaint, Decima had thought. Pretty in a way. If one liked that kind of thing.

It was odd how they had become such friends when they had nothing whatsoever in common, but Decima had been lonely and unhappy away from her father, and Rachel, separated from her parents for the first time, was kinder and more sympathetic than anyone else. Rachel's peaceful world of vicarage tea-parties and lawn tennis at weekends was such a different world from any Decima had ever known. For Decima was a child of high society, the daughter of a Scottish aristocrat and an Italian princess long since divorced, and until the age of fourteen Decima, in the custody of her erratic, volatile mother, had been shuttled to and fro across the continent and twice round the world while her mother took part in the endless social whirl of the current international set. And then her mother had died of an overdose of sleeping pills taken incontinently after a surfeit of alcohol, and Decima had been extricated from her cosmopolitan whirlpool and withdrawn by her father to the west coast of Scotland.

Decima had loved Ruthven from the first moment she had seen it. Her father had worried in case she had hated to come to such a backwater after the glamour of a dozen different cities, but to Decima, saturated with the sophistication of city life, Ruthven was a fairy-tale, a miraculous escape from that other world where she had been a forced onlooker at her mother's feverish pursuit of gaiety. She had loved it better than any place on earth.

Her father had been delighted by her marriage to Charles Mannering, an Oxford professor and author of two books on medieval history. He had liked Charles from the first, and had made him a trustee in administering Ruthven for Decima if she inherited the estate while still under age. He even inserted a clause to say that if Decima died before her twenty-first birthday the estate should pass to her children and, if there were no children, then title to the land should pass to Charles outright. But this was only to happen if Decima were to die before attaining her majority. Once she was twenty-one the trust ceased and the property became hers entirely to dispose of or retain as she wished. The house itself, being so remote, was in fact of little financial value, but the timber forests on the land were worth a small fortune and were leased to the Forestry Commission at an extremely profitable annual rate.

When her father died six months after her marriage, Decima found herself a wealthy heiress. She was nineteen at the time.

And now she was nearly twenty-one.

She sat for a long time on the window-seat that morning and stared out over the dark sea as she considered her problems. The difficulties were quite clear in her mind. It was the task of solving them which was so hard. Surely there must be some perfectly simple solution which was staring her in the face. It was a pity Rohan could not help her, but he was after all Charles' cousin. Rohan . . .

Rachel.

Decima was very still. If Rachel came, it might be the solution. Conventional, solid, dependable Rachel. It would be perfect. She had to come.

Moving swiftly over to the small secretaire in one corner of the room she found pen and paper and began to write in a small, neat, flowing hand.

II

Charles Mannering was sitting in his study which faced east to the mountains, and thinking of his wife. On his desk in front of him was a portrait of Decima on her wedding-day, and after a while he took the frame in his hands and stared at the picture for a long time. It was hard to believe it was a mere two and a half years since he had first seen her. But then it had been a very eventful two and a half years.

Leaning back in his chair he closed his eyes for a moment. He saw himself at thirty-six, a scholar highly regarded in intellectual circles, a bachelor snugly ensconced in his rooms at Oxford. He had almost everything he wanted by then, success in his work, personal freedom and a large circle of friends. It would have been entirely perfect, he had thought at the time, if he had had enough money to retire from teaching, which took up a good deal of his life, and to give him complete personal independence. He could have travelled, spent more time on research, had more time for writing books. But then one could not expect life to be entirely perfect, and he had on the whole been very fortunate. It would have been wrong to complain.

And then he had gone down to London one weekend to stay with his cousins, the Quists, and Rohan, with the air of a conjurer producing two white rabbits out of a top hat, had appeared triumphantly with two girls. He could remember vaguely seeing Rachel on a previous visit several years ago, but the other girl with her slanting blue eyes and silky black hair was unknown to him.

Of course she was absurdly young. It went without saying that a man of thirty-six would necessarily find a girl of eighteen a mere child. But suddenly after a few words with her he was struck with her sophistication and the knowledge which lay hidden in those slanting, watchful eyes. This girl was not as young as her years implied. There was something about her which was as old as time itself, and she knew it all too well.

Charles was fascinated, intrigued. He had always been attracted to older women before and this was the first time he had felt even a remote interest for a woman so young.

When he was sure he had not the slightest chance of being refused, he asked her to sleep with him.

Never had he more badly miscalculated. For one most unpleasant moment he thought he had ruined all his chances with her, but presently she forgave him and seemed anxious to see more of him. But any deviation from conventional morality was quite out of the question. If that was all he was interested in, he could forget about her.

Charles, like most clever men, fancied himself as being irresistible to women when he put his mind to it, and his *amour propre* had suffered a severe blow. In fact it was so badly bruised that on his return to Oxford he found it difficult to concentrate on his work and was completely unable to write any more of his book on *Richard Coeur de Lion*. Presently he sent a letter to Ruthven and received a charming reply inviting him up for the weekend. Charles was on the next plane to Inverness almost quicker than he could escape from his lecturing schedule.

He had liked Ruthven. Hopelessly primitive, of course, and completely impracticable (imagine having no road connecting it to the nearest town!) but a good place for a holiday and ideal for working quietly on a book or doing concentrated research. Decima's father, only a few years older than he, seemed a nice chap. He was pleased because he had just renewed the lease of part of his land to the Forestry Commission and thus insured a comfortable income for himself for the next few years. Useful things, trees. Timber was valuable these days. Since the coming of the Forestry Commission Ruthven's value had increased from barely two thousand to well over one hundred thousand pounds . . .

'I'm surprised you don't sell out,' Charles had said, thinking that so much money could be much more sensibly invested – a villa on the Costa Brava, perhaps, or a house in the Canary Islands. 'But then, of course,' he had added adroitly, 'it's your home and of great sentimental value to you.'

'Exactly!' said Decima's father, pleased that his guest should have understood his sentiments so well. 'Decima and I both feel the same way about that.'

'I quite understand,' said Charles, not understanding at all. 'I agree with you absolutely.'

Surely Decima could not really feel so attached to such a rambling, remote, ranshackle old house miles from anywhere! Decima with her background of international society, her education in Paris, Rome and Geneva – it was inconceivable that she could ever want to cling to this little corner of Western Scotland for any length of time. When she inherited the land she would no doubt change her mind about retaining it . . .

But she hadn't. That was what was so extraordinary. He replaced the photograph of her carefully on his desk and looked out of the window again at the bleak mountainside and moor which stretched to the forestry plantation. 'I'll never sell this,' she had told him bluntly, 'so you may as well forget about it. This is my home now and for all time.'

'But it's so remote, Decima!' he had protested. 'So cut off!

17

A young woman like you should travel and meet interesting people and—'

'I had enough travel when I was a child to last me a lifetime,' she had said, 'and I'm tired of meeting so-called interesting people. God, I have enough boring social life stuck down at Oxford with you in term-time, don't I? After a few weeks of that it's a relief to get back here.'

'I know you dislike the life at Oxford,' he had said carefully. 'God knows I'd be much happier if I didn't have to teach to supplement our income. But if I – you – were to sell Ruthven we could have enough money to invest to enable me to retire and we could easily settle in another part of Scotland near here—'

And she had said in contempt: 'I'm not selling Ruthven just so that you can live on my money for the rest of your life.'

It hurt even now to remember the tone of her voice. *I'm not selling Ruthven so that you can live on my money.* As if he were a gigolo or opportunist instead of a self-respecting Englishman with a great deal of pride.

Things had been very bad after that. They had gone for a whole week without speaking to one another and he had been miserable, unable to write or read, unwilling even to go fishing up the burn. But she hadn't cared. She had gone riding every day over the moors, or taken brief swims in the icy sea when the sun shone a little warmer than usual, and when the time had come to order the month's provisions she had taken the boat alone into Kyle of Lochalsh to do the shopping.

He could remember her very clearly coming back from the town. She wore a dark blue sweater which reflected the blue of her eyes and her dark hair was streaming behind her in the wind. He had never seen her look so beautiful or more hopelessly beyond his reach. And then as he came down to the jetty to help her unload the provisions she spoke to him for the first time since their quarrel a week ago and said:

'There's a letter for you. It's addressed in an exquisite gothic handwriting and the postmark is Cambridge.'

There was only one person who could be writing to him from

Cambridge in a gothic script. In the midst of his depression Charles was aware of pleasure, a quick pang of anticipation.

'Who is it from?' said Decima. 'I've never seen such a remarkable handwriting.'

'It's from a former student of mine,' he said mechanically. 'He went from Oxford on a scholarship to Cambridge to do postgraduate work; he's now making a study of the economic and social position of the monastic orders in England in the thirteenth century.' And even as he spoke he was ripping open the envelope and unfolding the single sheet of paper within.

'My dear Charles,' someone had written with elegant strokes of a pen dipped in black ink. 'My sister and I will shortly be in Edinburgh for the Festival, and I wondered if there was any possibility of meeting you there? Alternatively, if you do not intend to go to the Festival this year, I would very much like to visit you; Rebecca and I plan to hire a car after the Festival and see a little of Scotland, so it would be easy enough to drive up to Kyle of Lochalsh. If such a visit would inconvenience either you or your wife in any way, please don't hesitate to say so, but I would very much like to see you again and you always wrote such enthusiastic letters in praise of Ruthven that I find myself more than anxious to go there. Hoping, therefore, to see you again in the near future, I remain . . .' etc.

Charles folded the letter and put it away in his wallet.

'What's his name?' said Decima casually. 'Have I ever met him?'

'No,' said Charles. 'He left Oxford before I met you. His name is Daniel Carey.'

That had been two months ago. The Careys had now been six weeks at Ruthven and showed no sign of leaving.

Charles was still sitting in his study and thinking of the past when there was a soft knock on the door and the next moment a young woman of about twenty-four was slipping into the room. She hesitated as she saw he was deep in thought, and then as he looked across at her and smiled she stepped forward towards him.

'Am I interrupting anything?'

'No,' he said, still smiling. 'Sit down and talk to me for a while. I was just wondering how I could write of King John's obsession with the young Isabella of Angoulême without giving the impression I was writing a medieval version of *Lolita*.'

Rebecca laughed. 'You're teasing me as usual!'

'Why do you say that?'

'Historians of your calibre aren't concerned with the sexual obsessions of middle-aged potentates.'

Now it was his turn to laugh. 'Yet this particular infatuation had widespread consequences . . .' Really, he thought, looking at her, she was a most unusual girl. Possibly too intelligent for most men's tastes, but none the less attractive in a dark, fine-drawn, unusual way . . . And it was pleasant for once to talk to a woman who was well aware that Isabella of Castile and Isabella of Angoulême were very far from being the same person.

For some reason he thought of his cousin. Perhaps Rohan would take a fancy to her. On the whole he hoped not. Rohan was much too much of an extroverted young philistine to appreciate the fine qualities of a woman such as Rebecca Carey.

'Have you seen Decima this morning?' he inquired. 'I hope she hasn't forgotten that my cousin Rohan is arriving today.'

'No, she was talking of going into Kyle of Lochalsh to meet him this afternoon. I understand she has some shopping to do.'

'I see. And Daniel?'

'I believe he volunteered to go with her.'

'I see,' said Charles, and idly began to picture how he would spend the long peaceful afternoon at Ruthven . . .

III

When Rebecca left Charles she went upstairs to her bedroom and flung herself face downwards on the bed, her hands crushing the pillow fiercely and pulling it against her breast. Her whole body was trembling, alive with a million vibrations, and after a while she could lie still no longer but ran from her room and out of the house to the sea. The sun was warm; there was no one about and, if she had not seen the boat moored to the jetty, she would have assumed Decima and Daniel had already set off for Kyle of Lochalsh. Charles was no doubt still in his study which faced east over the mountains.

When she was about two hundred yards from the house she sank down behind a rock out of the wind and paused to regain her breath. For a moment she wondered whether to go swimming; the cold would be acute at first, she knew, but after a moment it would become more tolerable, and she loved fighting the high waves which pounded into surf on the deserted beach. She was just considering going back to the house for a towel and a bathing suit when she saw Daniel coming towards her across the sands.

Daniel was her only brother, and there were no sisters. Her parents had died soon after she was born; she could remember neither of them, only the cousins who had brought her up in Suffolk, near Bury St Edmunds. Consequently, because Daniel was the only close member of her family she had ever known, it was not surprising that she should have relied so much upon his companionship and derived such a sense of security from sharing his interests. As she had grown older she had conscientiously modelled herself on him, straining to keep up with all his interests and follow the development of his thoughts and philosophies. He liked to talk to her and all she wanted was to be a worthy companion to him on such occasions. She admired his mind so much that she felt it a compliment when he tried to share it with her. She was, after all, only his young sister. A lesser man would have ignored her or else merely talked to her in a patronizing manner, but when Daniel talked to her it was as if she were his equal.

She felt the most important person in the world on those occasions; she could even forget she was merely a thin, sallow girl with plain features and a moderate intellectual capacity which would always fall short of brilliance.

Her looks had improved as she entered her twenties and she found men were beginning to take an interest in her, but she had no patience with anyone less clever than herself and so her friendships never lasted long. Charles Mannering, however, was very different from the young men she was accustomed to discarding in impatient disappointment; she soon realized not only that Charles was exceptionally clever but also that he was the first man she had ever honestly admired – apart from Daniel, of course, but Daniel was only her brother. She wondered idly why Daniel had not yet married; there had been plenty of opportunities she knew, but no woman ever seemed to interest him for long.

As he came within earshot she called a greeting and he raised his hand in response, his footsteps soundless on the soft sand, the wind whipping the words from his mouth as he tried to reply. She saw him smile, shrug his shoulders in resignation; his dark eyes were narrowed against the sun, his hands thrust casually into the pockets of his trousers to confirm his air of nonchalance, and when he reached her a moment later his voice was low and cool and unhurried.

'Are you coming into Kyle of Lochalsh with us?' he asked. 'We're going in ten minutes.'

'No,' she said. 'There's nothing I want there.'

He looked at her for a moment and she had the feeling he could see right into her mind and knew exactly why she had no interest in going. Presently he said:

'You like it here, don't you? It's a pity you can't marry Charles and live here with him.'

'Ruthven doesn't belong to Charles.'

'It would if Decima died before she was twenty-one.'

'I hardly think she's likely to die within the next eight days!' Then, suddenly: 'How did you find that out?'

'She told me.' He turned aside. 'Are you sure there's nothing you want at Kyle of Lochalsh?'

'Quite sure, thanks, Danny.'

'I'll see you later, then,' he said and moved away from her on his way across the shore to the jetty. As she watched him, she saw Decima leave the house with a basket over her arm and step into the waiting motor-boat.

Decima always looked so smart. This afternoon she was wearing dark slacks and a pale blue sweater with a turtle-neck. Daniel too would think she looked smart. Rebecca always knew how Daniel would feel about women.

After a while she moved slowly back to the house. The sun

was already overcast, and she knew the best of the day was gone. For the first time she wondered vaguely what Charles' young cousin would be like and then, when she entered the house a moment later, she forgot about Rohan Quist until his arrival at Ruthven several hours later.

IV

Rohan was drinking Scotch and water in a pub overlooking the harbour when they arrived. He had reached the town an hour earlier after an uneventful journey from Inverness in the red Volkswagen, and after garaging the car had decided to have a drink to pass the time. He recognized the motor-boat at once as it nosed its way through the fishing boats to the quay, and he recognized Decima at the wheel almost as soon as he saw the boat, but the dark man in the black windcheater was a stranger to him, someone whom he had not expected to see.

He was conscious instantly and inexplicably of jealousy.

They moored the boat and stepped onto the quay. The man was not as tall as he had at first anticipated, but he had a broad, powerful build. Rohan's slight frame tautened. Instinctively his scalp started to prickle; if he had been a dog the hackles would have risen on the back of his neck, and yet there was no logic in his reaction, no reason for his distrust.

The man touched Decima's arm without taking it and they walked along the quay side by side. They were talking. Rohan saw Decima laugh.

Who was this man?

They came nearer and nearer. Within minutes they had reached the door of the pub and were walking inside to look for him, but he was still so absorbed with the force of his reaction that he made no move from his chair. He felt cold suddenly, chilled by a series of emotions he had never experienced before. It was as if he had felt someone walking over his grave.

'Why, there you are!' cried Decima. 'Silly thing, why didn't you call out when you saw us come in? How are you? It's such a long time since you've been up here.'

'Yes,' he said. 'It is.' But he wasn't looking at her. He was looking right past her over her shoulder but, even as she turned to make the introductions, the stranger stepped forward of his own accord and held out his hand.

'My name is Daniel Carey,' he said with an unexpectedly charming smile. 'Welcome back to Ruthven, Mr Quist.'

CHAPTER TWO

I

It was Thursday when Rachel arrived at Ruthven. She reached Kyle of Lochalsh in the early evening and found Rohan waiting for her at the little station. He wore two sweaters, a jacket and a pair of heavy tweed trousers, and still contrived to look cold.

'Decima's in the boat to avoid the current breeze from the Arctic,' he told her. 'I hope you brought your winter clothes with you, because if you haven't you'll freeze to death in twenty-four hours. The weather changed yesterday, and I've never been so cold in all my life . . . Is this your luggage? Okay, let's go . . . Yes, it was quite warm till yesterday and then the mist started to blow in from the sea and the thermometer dropped twenty degrees or so. I think it's more the damp than the actual cold that's so chilling – it seems to get right into your bones and stay there till you shiver it out again . . . Did you have a good journey?'

'Fair.' She followed him as he left the station, a suitcase in either hand, and as they walked out into the street the damp chill of the wind blew across the sea from Skye towards them. 'I can hardly believe Decima really lives right out here,' she said to Rohan, drawing up the collar of her raincoat. 'Decima of all people! I can only visualize her in town against sophisticated backgrounds. I can picture Charles playing the role of country gentleman but the very idea of Decima playing the outdoor country-tweeds type is too much for me altogether.'

'Yes?' said Rohan with vague interest. 'And yet, curiously enough, it's Charles who seems ill at ease in his role and Decima who seems perfectly relaxed and content at Ruthven . . . There's the boat across the harbour – can you make it out? And there's Decima in the wheelhouse – you can just see her blue jacket.'

They walked on and were soon at the jetty by the water's

edge. There were fishermen attending to their nets, white gulls soaring aloft on the wind currents, the sounds of water and Gaelic voices and the occasional throbbing of an engine. Rachel was aware of strangeness, as if she were a traveller in a foreign land. This remote corner of Britain might have been a thousand miles from the Britain she knew, the soft verdant slopes of the Surrey hills with their tall, swaying beech trees and blazes of gorse and rhododendron. A world removed from the graceful houses and shining roads and half-hour train service to the throbbing metropolis of London. Perhaps, she thought, it was not so strange that Decima should feel at home here while Charles did not; Decima, with her cosmopolitan upbringing, would see nothing strange and hostile about this land while Charles would always be conscious that he was an Englishman in foreign territory, an intellectual far removed from Oxford's spires, a product of civilization adrift among barbarous surroundings.

'Is Charles really so ill at ease here?' she asked Rohan curiously.

'Well, perhaps that's a slight exaggeration, because I know he enjoys fishing and the opportunity to work in peace, but I think he's always anxious to get back to Oxford after a while. I can see his point of view, God knows. This place is all very fine for a holiday but to remain here for any length of time would be too much of a good thing. That's why I'm surprised the Careys have stayed so long. They've been six weeks at Ruthven now.'

A gull screamed overhead and dipped towards the sea. The sun shone briefly through the clouds for a moment; the grey landscape seemed to glow in response, and then harden as the sun disappeared again.

'Who are the Careys?' said Rachel.

'Didn't Decima mention them in her letter? How odd! I would have thought she'd have been sure to mention them.'

'But who are they? Some friends of Charles?'

'My dear R., they're the most extraordinary couple – I can't imagine what on earth you'll make of them. Rebecca Carey is one of these frighteningly intellectual women with a curious dramatic intensity which I find rather unnerving. Everything she does, she does with a passionate zeal which quite takes one's breath away. Rather tiring, actually.'

'Not your type, from the sound of her!'

'Well, she could be if she had a sense of humour, but unfortunately she's too busy taking everything – including herself – much too seriously.'

'You mean,' said Rachel, 'she doesn't find your jokes amusing.'

'I mean nothing of the kind! All I was saying was—'

'Yes, I see. And what about her husband? Is he full of passionate humourless zeal too?'

'He's her brother, not her husband, and a former pupil of Charles now doing research at Cambridge.' Rohan was watching the boat. They were two minutes away from it now. Decima had caught sight of them, he noticed, and was waving to them.

'How dull,' said Rachel, waving back with a smile. 'Whatever made Charles invite them to Ruthven? Ah, here comes Decima! Lord, she looks prettier than ever and I feel so untidy and travelstained . . .'

Decima was already stepping off the boat and moving swiftly towards them. The wind tore for a moment at her black hair and she swept it out of her eyes with a laugh. She wore no make-up, and as the result of many weeks spent in the damp, moist climate of the Highlands, her complexion was flawless, her skin pale but not pallid, her cheeks faintly glowing with a mere trace of rose. She wore loose-fitting slacks and a bulky windcheater and still contrived to look beautiful.

'Raye! How lovely to see you!' She had a low, soft voice with a slight indefinable hint of a foreign accent. It was a voice which needed few words to convey whatever emotion she chose to put in it. 'I'm so glad you could come.'

There was no sign of nervousness, none of the anxiety which had shown itself so clearly in the hurried letter. She was composed, effortlessly poised. She might have been a mature woman nearly thirty instead of a girl not yet twenty-one.

'It's most exciting to be here,' said Rachel politely, suddenly

27

smitten with the full force of her inferiority complex. 'I've never been to the Highlands before.'

'All aboard!' sang out Rohan, detecting the stiltedness in her voice and at once rushing to the rescue. 'Next stop Ruthven! Do you want to take the wheel, Decima?'

'We'd soon be aground if *you* took it!' the girl retorted, and they laughed, the moment of awkwardness forgotten. 'Are you cold, Rachel? Do you want to go below to the cabin out of the wind? You must be so tired after your journey.'

And as Rachel hesitated, not wishing to appear unsociable but dreading the chill of the wind, Rohan said: 'I'll call you just before Ruthven comes into sight – go and sit in the cabin and peer through the portholes and sip some of Decima's best Scotch.'

'Yes,' said Decima, 'get her a drink, Rohan. I can manage up here once you've helped me cast off.'

'I'm sure you can,' said Rohan, and added to Rachel: 'Decima handles a boat as well as she drives a car – better than most men.'

Decima laughed. 'Only the British can say a woman's masculine and mean it as a compliment!'

'My dear Decima,' said Rohan, 'only a man who was blind, deaf and dumb could ever doubt your femininity . . . I'll be with you in a moment, Rachel. Go down to the cabin and make yourself at home.'

Rachel did as she was told. The cabin was warm and snug and had two bunks, one on either side of the gangway. As she sat down on the nearest one she was suddenly conscious of weariness, and leaning back against the wall of the cabin she closed her eyes for a moment as the engines roared into life. She could hear Rohan's voice shouting something, then a thud from somewhere on deck, and gradually she could feel the boat moving, swaying away from the jetty and out to sea.

She sat up and glanced out of the porthole. The harbour was already receding and Kyle of Lochalsh a mere huddled collection of grey stone buildings below the bare, grey mountains inland.

Footsteps clattered above her. 'Found the whisky yet?' said

Rohan, entering the cabin amidst a draught of cool air. 'No? You will have some, won't you?'

'Please.' She watched him take a bottle from a cupboard above the bunk and then go aft into the tiny galley for a glass and some drinking water. A minute later the liquid was fire in her throat and she was beginning to feel better.

She glanced out of the cabin again. There was nothing to be seen at all now except the rocky coast and the bleakness of the moors and hills inland. Once more the sun shone for a moment, and its light flickered fitfully over the dark landscape.

'How odd,' she said, 'to see no houses, no trees, no roads. It's almost unnerving. I must be more over-civilized than I thought I was.'

'I don't know about being over-civilized,' said Rohan. 'Even the Highlanders themselves find it oppressive – aren't they always drifting south to the lowlands and the towns? And you can understand why. Imagine trying to make a living from land like that! Even the crofters around Ruthven drifted south in the end with their sheep.'

'And yet in a way, it's very beautiful.'

'Certainly,' said Rohan, 'for a little while.' He went back into the galley to mix himself a drink. When he returned she moved up on the bunk so that he could sit down beside her, and she thought how curious it was that she, who was so often shy with men, should always be perfectly at ease when she was with him.

'Well,' she said with a smile, 'tell me all the details. What's been happening?'

He shrugged. 'Not too much. I've been fishing a few times on my own. Charles came with me once, but he's very involved in his book at the moment and I think he decided to fish more out of politeness than anything else.'

'And have you been riding with Decima?'

'No,' he said, taking a gulp of his Scotch. 'But I've been out a couple of times alone – and nearly galloped into Cluny Sands without realizing I'd come so far. For God's sake don't go riding on your own, Rachel – if you ride inland you'll probably get lost on the moors and if you ride along the seashore you'll go straight into dangerous quicksands. You won't even know

29

they're quicksands till your horse starts to flounder. They look so white and beautiful and inviting, just like any other stretch of deserted sea-shore around here.'

'Why didn't Decima go with you? I'm sure she'd have kept you out of dangerous territory.'

'She seems to have lost interest in riding lately.'

'So you've been having a solitary sort of holiday!' she teased. 'Charles won't fish with you and Decima won't go riding! What about the Careys?'

'They don't ride or fish.'

'No? What on earth have they been doing with themselves for six weeks, then?'

'Rebecca swims.'

'*Swims*? In this climate?'

'It was warmer a little while ago. And she spends the rest of the time reading Jean-Paul Sartre and imagining herself to be a second Simone de Beauvoir.'

'And her brother?'

'Daniel? I really don't know. I never seem to see much of him.' He offered her a cigarette and gave her a light. 'I think I'll just see how Decima's managing on deck,' he said suddenly, standing up. 'We can't be too far from Ruthven by now. I'll be back in a minute.'

She was just closing her eyes in a moment of drowsiness a short while later when he called down the hatch to her. Rousing herself with an effort, she left the cabin and went up on deck.

The wind struck the side of her face as soon as she stepped outside the deck-house, and she felt her body tighten in an attempt to lock out the cold. The sea was a swaying grey shot with white flecks and the sky was a pale ragged blue streaked with banks of stormy clouds. At the wheel Decima's face was glowing, her long hair streaming behind her, her eyes bright, and beside her Rohan, hunched in his coat, called out something which was lost in the hum of the engine and the roar of the wind.

Rachel turned to face the wind, and as she did so, the boat rounded the peninsula and she saw Ruthven.

The wind whipped at the foam; there was salt on her lips,

spray in her eyes, a mist of water billowing from the prow of the boat. And through it all, there were the turrets and towers of Ruthven, grey walls clearly etched against the vast background of the moors, while beyond the walls, seemingly encroaching almost to the water's edge to the north and south of the bay, were the mountains wreathed in billowing mist.

Decima was at her elbow suddenly; Rohan had taken the wheel.

'Isn't it beautiful?' she said, and her eyes blazed with a passion which Rachel had never seen her show for any man. 'Isn't it the most perfect place in all the world?' And as she laid her hand on Rachel's arm, Rachel could feel the nervous strength flowing through those slim fingers, the vibrant tremor of joy.

'It's unique, Decima,' she heard herself say. 'I've never seen anything like it before.'

The landscape was so powerful that it was almost overwhelming. She wondered if she had ever felt as far from civilization as she felt at that moment, and the pang of fear, unexpected and ridiculous, made her stiffen for a moment before she pulled herself together.

Decima had returned to the wheel; as they approached the shore, Rachel could see the house more clearly, the rugged stone, the blank, dark windows, the partially cultivated garden. There was a jetty with a boat-house, stables and out-buildings beyond the house. A cow nibbled tranquilly in a grassy field to the right, and six little pigs frolicked in an enclosure beyond the cow. Hens wandered near the front door, and an enormous St Bernard who was snoozing on the porch with lofty disregard for fowls, opened his eyes at the sound of the motorboat and began to pad down towards the jetty.

The domesticity of the scene in close-up was oddly reassuring after the wildness of the long-distance view.

The boat curved towards the jetty, nudged it neatly and swayed to a halt as the motors died. The enormous dog put out a paw and patted it vaguely.

'Careful, George,' said Decima, jumping down onto the jetty and turning to help Rachel. 'Rohan, can you manage those suitcases? I can see Charles coming, so he'll be able to give you a hand with them.'

Rachel scrambled onto the jetty. The damp air felt deliciously cool and fresh now that they were out of the wind. She took a deep breath, half-closing her eyes, and when she looked up again she saw Decima's husband crossing the sands towards them.

There was a girl with him, a dark young woman in a thick green sweater and a tweed skirt.

'That's Rebecca Carey,' said Decima's voice carelessly. 'I don't think I mentioned to you that we had guests at Ruthven, did I, Raye?'

'Rohan told me.'

The St Bernard rose with vast dignity and advanced towards Charles. His bulk filled the jetty.

'Out of the way, George,' Rachel heard Charles say good-naturedly. 'That's better . . . Why, Rachel, how very nice to see you again! Did you have a good journey? You did? Splendid . . . May I introduce you to one of our guests? Rebecca, this is Rachel Lord. Rachel – Rebecca Carey.'

The girl's hand was limp. Rachel took it but soon let it go. 'How do you do?' she said politely.

Something else had caught the attention of the St Bernard. He was plodding majestically over the sands and his long tail was waving with unhurried grace.

'Can I give you a hand with those suitcases, Rohan?'

'. . . come up to the house. All right?'

'. . . sea's a bit choppy . . .'

'Not so good for swimming, Rebecca! Decima, why don't you . . .'

A man had come out of the house and was walking down towards them to the beach. When he reached the St Bernard, he paused to put a finger lightly on the dog's head and the dog looked up at him as if that one caress signified immeasurable honour.

'This way, Rachel,' said Decima, walking along the jetty away from the boat.

The man and the dog reached the edge of the sands together.

The St Bernard was moving surprisingly fast without giving the appearance of making any extra effort. The man, though, was moving slowly yet gave the impression of speed. He wore a dark pullover and dark trousers and his hair was as dark as his eyes.

'Ah, there you are!' said Decima, and her voice rang out across the sands. 'I was wondering where you'd gone to!' She turned to Rachel, and her eyes were as vivid as a southern sky in high summer. 'This is Rebecca's brother, Raye,' she said. 'This is Daniel Carey.'

II

Daniel saw a tall, slim girl with soft brown hair and shy eyes and a wide, beautiful mouth. Because he was an observant man he also noticed that she was badly dressed in a raincoat which did not suit her, and wore ugly shoes in a style which might just possibly have been fashionable some years previously. Her smile was hesitant but full of warmth, and he knew at once that she was honest and would find any insincerity distasteful. Beside her, Decima's poised brilliance seemed strangely artificial and cold, an exercise in perfection which was as empty as it was unarousing.

'Have you much luggage, Miss Lord?' he asked her, scrupulously polite. 'Can I help bring it up to the house?'

'Charles and Rohan are seeing to that,' said Decima before Rachel could speak. 'Come on up to the house with us, Daniel.'

Perhaps it was her tone of voice which made him at once want to do exactly the reverse of any suggestion she happened to make, or perhaps he was too conscious of the knowledge that she did not attract him at that moment and that he wanted to escape from her. Whichever it was, he stepped past them towards the jetty and called back over his shoulder: 'I'll just see if there's anything I can do.'

The St Bernard lumbered after him placidly, brushing Rachel's raincoat with his waving tail.

'George!' called Decima sharply.

But the dog pretended not to hear her.

'I can't think why George likes you so much, Daniel,' observed Charles descending from the jetty with one of Rachel's suitcases. 'You never pay any attention to him.'

'You sound almost jealous, Charles!' said Rohan from behind him. He was smiling, but the smile never reached his eyes. 'I thought you were above feeling jealous of things in your possession.'

My God, thought Daniel. This is a stupid man.

He felt himself go ice-cold with rage.

But Charles was laughing, deaf to all insinuations, happily oblivious of any emotional undercurrents in the atmosphere. 'I wouldn't grudge anyone a dog's affection! But I've never known George to be so friendly towards a stranger before – Daniel must have a way with animals, I suppose.'

'Daniel has a way with all kinds of things,' said Rohan Quist, but Charles had moved on down the jetty and wasn't listening to him.

Rebecca spun round. 'What's that supposed to mean?'

'He's merely paying tribute to my many talents,' said Daniel very quickly before Quist could open his mouth. 'Let's go back to the house.'

As they stepped off the jetty, Rebecca began to say something to him but he cut her off abruptly with a single movement of his hand and she was silent at once. Really, he thought in irritation. Rebecca was unusually sensitive these days. Dangerously sensitive, in fact. He must have a word with her later.

When they reached the house he went into the living-room while the others took the luggage upstairs, and moved over to the sideboard to mix himself a drink. He had just gone over to the window with his drink in his hand when his sister came into the room.

'Shut the door, please.'

She shut it. 'Danny—'

'What's the matter with you?' he said angrily. 'Why couldn't you have ignored Quist altogether? You played right into his hands!'

'But Danny, when he said—'

'Ignore it. Forget it. Can't you get into the habit of ignoring anything Quist says which might conceivably have a *double entendre*?'

'But—'

'He's out to make trouble, that man – you know that as well as I do. Why give him the satisfaction of knowing he's succeeding?'

'But Danny, supposing Charles—'

'The hell with Charles!' said Daniel, and then stopped dead as Charles walked into the room.

Quist was right behind him.

'Can I get either of you a drink?' he heard himself offer, giving them his most charming smile.

'Thank you,' said Rohan, 'but no.'

'Charles? Will you drink some Scotch on the rocks with me?'

'Thanks,' said Charles cheerfully. 'That's exactly what I need.' He sat down in a chair and stretched out his legs before the hearth in a picture of relaxed ease. 'What about you, Rebecca?' he added. 'Will you have a drink?'

'Not at present, thank you, Charles.' Her voice was taut and uneasy.

There was a silence. Daniel served cubes from the ice-bucket into the glass, and stirred the whisky carefully without any apparent trace of tension.

'Here you are, Charles,' he said at last, turning to face his host, and even as he spoke he wondered if Charles was really unaware of Rohan's attitude, of Rebecca's nervousness, of his own mixed emotions of disillusionment, scorn and contempt. Daniel had a sudden painful memory of those days not so long ago when he had been a freshman at Oxford and had waited eagerly to gain admission to the hall where the celebrated historian Charles Mannering was lecturing. It was hard to believe it was such a short time since he had admired and respected Charles. No doubt, Daniel thought, it would have been different if he and Rebecca had never come to Ruthven.

Ruthven had changed everything.

The silence was threatening to become prolonged again when the door opened and Decima came into the room.

'Why, how quiet it is in here!' She was so poised, so apparently unaware that anyone should be ill at ease in that plain, cheerful room that her very presence seemed to mock the tension among them. Rohan said, 'I think I will have a drink after all,' and Charles was already reaching for his pipe; over by the window Rebecca picked up an old magazine to take over to the armchair in the corner, while Daniel sat down opposite Charles by the hearth with the massive St Bernard at his feet.

'Dinner will be in about an hour,' said Decima. 'I thought that would give Rachel sufficient time to have a bath and change and recover a little after her long journey.'

The talk became desultory; after a while Decima departed to see if the cook was coping satisfactorily with the meal, and soon after she returned Rachel came downstairs from her room to join them. She was wearing a grey dress in a style that was too old for her, and a plain elegant brooch which even the best-dressed woman in the world would have been pleased to wear. Her short hair had been carefully brushed and shone in the ray of sunlight which slanted into the room. She still looked shy.

Everyone made a great fuss of her, Daniel thought. Charles immediately offered her a drink. Rohan insisted that she sit next to him on the couch. Decima immediately assumed the role of perfect hostess, anxious, solicitous, exerting every surreptitious means to make her guest perfectly relaxed and at ease.

He still couldn't understand why Decima had suddenly invited her to Ruthven.

'. . . haven't really had the chance to talk to you about the celebrations for my twenty-first,' Decima was saying with animation. 'It's all rather exciting – I'm so glad you could come, Raye – I do hope you'll enjoy it . . .'

The birthday party seemed to have given Decima an excellent excuse for issuing her unexpected invitation. But an excuse for what?

'. . . Charles is giving a dinner-party for me on Saturday. There'll be sixteen guests and we'll light the fires in the hall and get out the long dining-table and if Willie – that's the game-keeper – and the men have luck shooting, we'll be able to roast venison on the spit . . .'

Daniel thought of his own twenty-first birthday five years

earlier on the eve of his last term at Oxford. There had been a party which had made the Dean blanch and the townsfolk complain, and he had almost decided to get married. Luckily, even in spite of a surfeit of champagne, he had avoided committing himself. The next morning a letter had arrived from his parent's lawyers to the effect that he was now fully entitled to the money which had been held in trust for him since childhood.

Decima would come into money too, of course. And, once she was twenty-one, she could do as she pleased with Ruthven.

'Who will the sixteen guests be?' the girl was asking.

'Oh, Rebecca and Daniel, of course, you and Rohan, Charles and I – and the MacDonalds and Camerons from Kyle of Lochalsh, and the Kincaids from Skye, and my father's lawyer, old Mr Douglas of Cluny Gualach and his daughter Rosalind; we had to ask Mr Douglas as he wrote me an enormously long legal letter the other day all about my father's will and inheriting all the money and all the sordid little details about that . . .'

'You would hardly describe the ownership of Ruthven as a sordid little detail, would you, Decima?' Daniel could not resist saying.

'Well, no, I agree!' She laughed carelessly, took a sip from her glass. 'But lawyers somehow succeed in taking the romance out of becoming twenty-one and reduce it to such mundane levels . . . May I have some more wine, Charles?'

Daniel wondered idly if Decima was aware that she drank too much. The preliminary glasses hardly seemed to affect her, and even after that the effect was barely noticeable.

In contrast, the other girl scarcely seemed to touch her wine at all. Yet she appeared to enjoy the meal, for she smiled often and seemed to lose much of her reserve. Once or twice she glanced at him and caught him watching her, and he saw her blush faintly after she had looked away and pretended to interest herself in something else.

He wondered what kind of relationship she had with Rohan Quist, but decided it was probably true that there was nothing between them except ordinary friendship. Quist, even though only a year younger than Daniel himself, seemed a mere child still, excitable, over-emotional and immature, and those qualities were hardly sufficient to attract any woman, let alone a woman with such unusual simplicity of manner as Rachel Lord.

When she and Decima rose at last to leave the men alone with their liqueurs, he realized to his astonishment that he had been thinking about her continually throughout the meal, and as he watched her leave the room, he was aware of wondering curiously whether she too had been thinking of him.

III

Rachel excused herself early, saying that she was tired after the long journey and, with a lamp in her hand, found her way up the curving staircase to her room. Someone, presumably the housekeeper, had lit the fire in the grate and the flames had already taken the chill from the air, but outside the rain hurtled in from the Atlantic and dashed itself against the windowpane, and as she knelt on the hearth to warm her hands she could hear the wind rasping against the outer walls.

It was strange to remember that it was only September and that, far away in the south, people would be wearing summer clothes and perhaps taking a stroll in the evening sunlight.

The wind hummed through the eaves again; she shivered and drew closer to the warmth of the fire.

The flames were flickering, spiralling columns of light, distorted patterns, fragments of vitality. She stared at them for a long time, and as she watched she thought of Daniel Carey and wondered why it was that she was so shy with men and lacked all trace of her usual self-confidence. With any man whom she did not know she was always painfully ill at ease.

Carey had no doubt thought her very gauche.

She was just recalling Decima's perfect poise and maturity of manner, and thinking that self-confidence was undoubtedly easy if one happened to be beautiful, when there was a knock on the door. At first she thought she was imagining it or confusing it with the soughing of the rain and wind outside, but even as she started and turned her head uncertainly towards the door, the knock came again.

'Rachel?' said a soft voice urgently, and the next moment the door was opening and Decima was slipping into the room. 'Ah, there you are.' She shut the door behind her and moved swiftly over to the hearth where Rachel was still sitting. 'Thank God I've at last got a chance to talk to you alone.'

Rachel looked blank, and then realized she had been so absorbed in remembering the conversations at dinner that she had temporarily forgotten the letter which had brought her to Ruthven.

'I've been waiting for a chance to talk to *you* alone,' she said lightly to Decima. 'What on earth were you hinting at in your letter? I couldn't make head or tail of it except that you seemed to be in a rather panic-stricken state – and yet here you are as cool as a cucumber and just as balanced as you always were! Just what exactly's going on?'

Decima had a fur stole over the midnight-blue dress she had worn at dinner, and as she sat down on the floor beside Rachel she drew the stole more closely round her shoulders. Her face looked white and pinched suddenly; the firelight flickered across the violet circles beneath her eyes and glinted in an expression which made mockery of Rachel's light, amused remarks.

Rachel suddenly felt her heart beating uncertainly, and the shock of recognition prickled beneath her scalp. 'Something's very wrong,' she heard herself say. 'That's it, isn't it, Decima? Something's very wrong.'

Decima didn't answer.

'Tell me what it is.'

There was a silence. And then as the wind sighed again in the eaves and the rain hissed in the darkness beyond, she heard Decima whisper:

'I think Charles is planning to kill me.'

CHAPTER THREE

I

The fire was still dancing, wrapping greedy tongues of red and yellow around the logs. And the light danced on Decima's face so that the fear shone in her eyes and her knuckles gleamed white as she clasped her hands tightly together.

Rachel said: 'Charles?'

'I've suspected it for some while.'

Rachel's mind at that moment seemed incapable of anything except recalling odd random memories. She thought of Geneva where she had first met Decima and how little she had suspected at the time that the meeting would lead to this moment at Ruthven years later; she thought of the spires of Oxford and an adolescent Rohan boasting of his celebrated cousin Charles; she thought of her first meeting with Charles Mannering, the occasion when he had first seen Decima; she thought of his charm and erudition, his wisdom and wit, his vanity and conceit and pride.

It came as a shock to realize fully, for the first time, how much she had always disliked him!

'You can't believe it, can you?' Decima was saying. 'You can't believe that it could ever be true. You've only seen Charles in his role of academic celebrity, respected and admired by countless intellectuals, the pillar of Oxford society, the perfect English gentleman. You don't believe, do you, that he could ever be otherwise than charming and good-natured and generous.'

'I—'

'Well, I didn't believe it either! When I married him he seemed everything I could ever want, an older man whom I could trust and lean upon, a clever man whom I could respect, the kind, considerate husband I felt sure could make me happy. But I was wrong. He never loved me! He married me because of my looks, because I would cause a stir wherever I went in Oxford and he could bask in my reflected glory and listen to other men congratulate him on his wife! I soon discovered how selfish and vain he was, soon realized that the only person *he* cared about was himself! However, I too was proud and I didn't want to run to my father and admit that I'd made a terrible mistake in marrying this man, so I said nothing and pretended all was well when all the time disillusionment followed disillusionment and I wished to God I'd never met him.'

There was a silence. The warmth of the firelight seemed strangely incongruous in contrast to the stormy darkness without and Decima's low unsteady voice close at hand.

'But it wasn't until after my father died, that I realized the main reason why Charles married me. I can't think why I never saw it before – I must have been blind, but it wasn't until Father was dead and the lawyers were trying to decide what his will meant, that I realized Charles had married me for my money.

'Charles is basically very lazy. He's not interested in teaching students – or in doing any formal work! He pretends he likes free time to write and do research, but he doesn't write much! He just enjoys being a gentleman of leisure, and if I sold Ruthven and invested the proceeds, he'd never have to teach again. When he married me he thought I'd sell it as soon as I reached twenty-one – he couldn't conceive that I could ever really *like* living here, that I wouldn't sell it for all the money in the world. He didn't understand what it meant to me to have a home I loved after so many years of traipsing from one hotel to the next with my mother throughout my childhood. He made no pretence of even trying to understand. He was angry because he wanted the money and I was quite determined that it should never get into his hands.

'I don't suppose you have any idea of the terms of my father's will. My father, like everyone else, was deceived by Charles' superficial charm and thought he would be the ideal person to look after my interests if I was left an orphan before I was twenty-one; so in his will, my father made Charles, as well as the lawyer Mr Douglas and his partner, a trustee of his estate if he died leaving me a minor. He inserted a clause to say that if I died before I was twenty-one the estate should pass to my children, and if I had no children then it should pass to Charles. If I died after I was twenty-one, and had left no will disposing of the estate as I wished, Ruthven would still pass to Charles as my next-of-kin.'

'And have you made a will?'

'It's all drafted and ready to be signed as soon as I'm twenty-one. I have to be twenty-one before I can make a valid will, as I expect you know. But if I die before I'm twenty-one, the terms of the trust will come into effect and Ruthven will pass to Charles. There's nothing I can do to alter that.'

'Has he already tried to force you to sell it?'

'Soon after my father died Charles tried to urge the other trustees to sell on my behalf, but they wouldn't when they knew I was very much opposed to the idea of the sale. As trustees they have a power of sale, but in practice they would never force a sale without my consent. Mr Douglas was an old friend of my father's.'

'So—'

'Charles wants Ruthven – or rather the money that the sale of Ruthven would bring him. He knows damn well that I would never leave him a square inch of it in any will I might make after I'm twenty-one, and so his only chance to acquire it would be if I were to die before my twenty-first birthday.'

'But Decima, your birthday's Saturday and this is Thursday evening—'

'My birthday's on Sunday. The dinner-party is on Saturday so that everyone can drink my health as the clock strikes twelve and my birthday officially begins. The idea was Charles', not mine.'

'But that means he has only forty-eight hours left—'

'That's why I invited you to Ruthven – because I couldn't face it any longer on my own. My nerves weren't strong enough, and there was no one I could trust—'

'Not even Rohan?'

'Charles' cousin?' said Decima ironically. 'No, I wouldn't trust Rohan.'

'And the Careys?'

'I don't trust the Careys,' said Decima.

'Why? Because they're Charles' friends?'

'Because they've outstayed their welcome without any apparent reason and are both determined to stay until after my twenty-first birthday party . . . Because Charles likes them and begged them to stay. Because . . . of many things.' She looked into the flames, and her eyes were bright and hard. 'Rebecca is the kind of woman I despise, and Daniel—'

She stopped.

'Daniel?'

'Daniel isn't interested in women,' said Decima. 'History and learning and books are all he cares about. Do you think he would listen even if I did tell him my suspicions about Charles? Of course not. He would smile politely but think me a mere neurotic female highly unworthy of any attention he could spare me . . . And anyway, I could never confide in Daniel.'

'But Decima, has Charles made any move, given you any hint that he might try to—'

'He hasn't mentioned selling Ruthven since the Careys came,' Decima interrupted. 'That in itself is unusual. And his behaviour in general has been strange. He's been so extraordinarily nice to me! He really has taken trouble over the dinner-party arrangements, and he's promised to give me a beautiful diamond necklace for my birthday (which he can't afford, incidentally), and he's even suggested—' She bit her lip and glanced at Rachel from beneath her lashes. 'We haven't lived together for over a year,' she said after a moment, glancing back into the flames. 'Recently I've been locking my door at night when I go to bed. Charles suggested that I started sleeping in his room again as I did when we were first married.'

'But—'

'And he has debts,' she said suddenly, as if rushing away from a subject she had no wish to discuss. 'I – I looked among his papers once when he was out fishing . . . We lived far beyond our income after we were first married – I think he was relying on the money from Ruthven's sale to help him with the bills . . . He has even borrowed money to pay his earlier debts.

43

And yet he talks of buying me a diamond necklace as if he had all the money in the world! Besides, we're always quarrelling over money. Before the Careys came we used to quarrel almost every other day and the subject of Ruthven's sale was always cropping up.'

'Why should the Careys' arrival make him drop the subject, I wonder?'

'I don't know, but I think he has some scheme, and the Careys have some leading part in it. I don't know why else he would drop the subject entirely, unless he had decided that reasoning with me was useless and it was necessary to make other plans.'

'Have you never thought of leaving Ruthven? You must have been very frightened these last few days.'

'Of course I've thought of it! But there are two things which have always deterred me. The first is simply that I've no proof that Charles is planning violence and it *is* possible that I may be mistaken about his intentions – this doesn't reverse anything I've just said against him, because I'm still convinced he married me for my money and would love to get his hands on it. But I've no tangible proof that he plans to kill me. Supposing I was wrong? If I left him now when he may well be genuinely eager to be generous towards me and to organize such lavish celebration for my birthday, I don't think a judge would be very sympathetic if I tried to get a divorce; Charles won't divorce me. It would reflect too badly on his ego and pride – to have to confess that he, the great success, had made a failure of marriage, and couldn't hold on to his much-displayed wife! And with his job and background he's not going to smear himself by providing the evidence for any adultery petition of mine. My one hope of a divorce is being able to prove he drove me into desertion. Besides, who knows? If he is innocent and I've misjudged him, perhaps the situation may improve once I'm twenty-one and he no longer has a hope of getting his hands on my money . . . But perhaps I'm expecting too much. Certainly, as things stand at the moment that's a hopelessly optimistic view.'

'I see . . .'

'My other reason for staying is minor in comparison but not unimportant. Ironic though it may seem, at present I've no money of my own and couldn't afford to go away – all my income from the Forestry Commission is used by the trustees in seeing to Ruthven's upkeep and giving me a ridiculously small allowance; the balance is put into the trust fund for me to inherit when I'm twenty-one.'

'So Charles can't even borrow money from you?'

'He can get nothing whatsoever unless I die before midnight on Saturday.'

Rachel stared at her. 'But Decima—' She paused, trying to marshal her thoughts into a sensible pattern and ignore the knowledge that she was far from the protective shields of civilization, but the howl of the wind and the hammering of the rain outside seemed to undermine her reserves of strength with horrifying thoroughness. She could only think that she was ten miles by sea from the nearest town, imprisoned between the vast mountains and the stormy sea, and that the danger in that still house suddenly seemed immensely alive and vital: This was no half-imagined illusion conjured up by any neurosis of Decima's; this was a reality in which she herself was personally involved. 'But what can I do?' she whispered to Decima. 'Tell me what I can do.'

'Stay with me. Don't leave me alone with Charles. And be on your guard for me.'

'Why, yes . . . of course. It'll only be till Sunday, won't it? Once you're twenty-one, you're no longer in danger because Charles would have nothing to gain from your death.'

There was a silence. At last Decima glanced at her watch, 'I must go back before they start wondering why I'm staying here so long . . . I shall go down and tell them I feel tired and have decided to follow your example in going to bed early. Then I'll go to my room and lock my door and try and get some sleep.'

'Would you like to sleep in here? One of us could sleep on the couch . . . But no, I suppose that would cause suspicion if we were found out.'

'Yes, I think so, and I want to avoid letting Charles know I'm

45

afraid and suspect him of anything . . . Once he thinks I suspect something, he'll be on his guard.'

'Didn't he think it suspicious that you'd asked me to stay when we'd more or less lost touch with each other?'

'No, you were a friend of Rohan's and he thought inviting you was a clever idea on my part to make the numbers even for the dinner-party . . . Oh, and he was probably glad you could come because he would feel you would divert Rohan's attention from me.' She stood up, automatically straightening her dress, her fingers working nervously over the material. 'Charles is convinced that Rohan and I are having an affair,' she said with a laugh which held no trace of mirth. 'Amusing, isn't it? As if I would! Anyway, I'd be more than glad if you could occupy Rohan for me, if only to allay Charles' ridiculous suspicions . . . Now I really must go – I'll see you tomorrow morning, of course. Perhaps you'd like to have breakfast with me in my room at nine-thirty? Mrs Willie, the housekeeper, always brings breakfast up to me in the mornings . . . And thank you for listening to me so well, Raye – I feel better already, just through talking about all my fears and worries to someone . . . Till tomorrow, then – I hope you sleep well, by the way. Do you have everything you want here?'

'Yes, I think so, thanks. Goodnight, Decima – and try not to worry too much.'

Decima smiled faintly; there was a draught as she opened the door and the next moment her footsteps were receding down the passage and Rachel was alone once more by the fire in the darkened room.

She threw another log into the flames. Sparks flew up the chimney. She sat for a long time while watching the wood burn and then very slowly she began to get undressed. But even as she got into bed sometime later and drew the blankets tightly around her, she found she was still wondering what part Daniel Carey played in any plans Charles might have for Decima's future.

When she awoke the sun was shining through the curtains and, on moving to the window, she saw that the sea was a rich, dark, swaying blue which stretched to the clear line of the horizon. The sky was pale and cloudless, bearing no trace of the stormy evening before, and the white sands shone invitingly in the light of early morning.

It was eight o'clock, long before the time for the promised breakfast with Decima at nine-thirty. The memory of Decima and the conversation of the previous evening made her pause motionless by the window for several long seconds and then, on realizing she was cold, she retreated to the warmth of her bed once more.

But she was uneasy, restless. After a time she recognized the impossibility of falling asleep again, and she got up, found a pair of slacks and a thick sweater, and started to get dressed. Within ten minutes she was slipping out into the corridor. At the head of the stairs she paused to listen but the house was quiet and she supposed everyone else was still sleeping. She reached the hall. She could hear faint sounds now, but they came from the kitchens far away where the housekeeper was already at work. Moving in the other direction, Rachel opened the front door and stepped into the clear cool air outside.

The landscape seemed different in sunshine. As she walked downhill towards the jetty she could see that the mountains beyond the house were shimmering in green and purple shades, and now that there was no mist covering the scene she could see the dark line of the trees forming the edge of the forestry plantation far away across the moors. Above the jetty she paused to look around her; to the left the sands stretched south along the black cliffs which rose abruptly from the harbour of Ruthven, and to the right the sands were curtained by the rocky arm of a peninsula thrusting out into the ocean.

Rachel turned south.

The breeze was cool, but no longer damp and chill. The sunlight, though pallid, was faintly warm. Gulls swooped above the roar of the surf and soared high over the black cliffs, and their screams carried shrilly on the air currents to echo among the rocks.

Rachel was conscious suddenly of loneliness. She glanced back over her shoulder at the house, but Ruthven was gone, hidden by a jutting corner of the cliffs, and there was no sign of civilization. She hesitated uneasily, and then pulled herself together with a smile at her city-dweller's reactions and walked on.

The cliffs were taller now, great scarred walls of granite with rocks piled at their base and embedded in the sand. There were caves too, some enormous caverns the size of a church, some mere holes barely high enough for upright stance. Rachel, venturing nearer the cliff-face, found deep pools left behind by the tide and an assortment of shell-fish and seaweed clustered in the water among the rocks.

She was just stooping to examine a large shell when she suddenly felt she was being watched. She swung round abruptly, but there was nothing there, only the roar of the surf and the screaming of the gulls. Her heart was pounding in her lungs so hard that even her movements away from the cliffs were stiff and awkward, but once she was close to the breaking waves and away from the dark, gaping mouths of the caves she felt better. She started walking again and soon she had rounded another rocky peninsula and was standing before another expanse of wide white sands, unmarked, untouched, effortlessly beautiful. She stepped out towards them quickly, forgetting her absurd nervousness of a few minutes before and feeling unexpectedly light-hearted.

There was a howl from behind her. An enormous throaty baying echoed among the cliffs and as she spun round in shock she saw the vast St Bernard pounding towards her, his jaws gaping as he bared his teeth.

Like most people unaccustomed to even small dogs, Rachel was too frightened to move. And then as the dog reached her and she stepped back automatically in self-defence, she felt her heels sinking and realized in a flash of understanding that she

48

had wandered right to the very edge of the quicksands of Cluny.

She froze in her tracks, and the dog stopped too, still baying in warning. Then, very delicately he stepped forward, tail swaying and took the cuff of her jacket between his teeth to lead her away from the sands to safety. Rachel automatically wrenched her shoes free to follow him, and presently the dog released his hold on her jacket and looked up at her sadly as if incredulous that anyone could be so stupid and careless.

She was just stroking the top of the dog's head when she saw Daniel.

He was standing at the entrance to one of the caves, but as she saw him he began to walk over to her. He walked slowly, not hurrying, his hands in the pockets of his old dark corduroys, and when he drew nearer she saw that his eyes were watchful and his mouth was unsmiling.

'Did no one tell you,' he said, 'about Cluny Sands?'

'Why, yes,' she said, stumbling over the words just as she had always done at school. 'Yes, Rohan told me. But I didn't think – I didn't remember –'

'I see.' He whistled to the dog. 'Here, George.'

The St Bernard lumbered over to him obediently and sat down on the sand, his tail still swaying.

'Why didn't you call out to me sooner?' Rachel heard herself demand. 'Why did you let me get right to the edge before you sent the dog after me?'

'I thought you were certain to know about the sands and would stop before you reached the edge. Besides, the tide's out and the sands are less dangerous; the danger comes when the tide is on the turn.' He was still motionless and there was something about his eyes which brought her back to the raw-ness of adolescent emotions, a world she thought she had outgrown long ago.

She glanced away out to sea. 'I still think you might have called out sooner,' she said abruptly.

Some indefinable element in his manner was at once erased; he smiled, and his voice when he spoke was full of charm and warmth.

'I do apologize,' he said. 'It was wrong of me, I see that now, and you must have had a bad shock. Let me take you back to the house and brew you some coffee to make amends.'

She glanced at him briefly but lowered her eyes even before she smiled in return. 'Thank you,' she murmured. 'But I'm quite all right.'

'But you'll accept my offer of coffee all the same, I hope.'

'I – I've promised to have breakfast with Decima.'

'Decima never looks at a breakfast tray before nine-thirty,' said Daniel, 'and we'll be back at the house long before that. However, it's as you wish, of course.' His shoe knocked against a pebble and he stooped to pick it up and fling it out to sea. 'How do you find Decima, by the way? Has she changed much since you last saw her?'

'No, she doesn't seem to have changed. But then I've hardly seen her yet.'

'You never actually knew her very well, did you?'

'Why, yes,' said Rachel, astonished enough to glance up into his eyes. 'I knew her very well indeed! We were at school in Geneva together for nine months and were the closest of friends.'

'Oh?' said Daniel. 'You surprise me.'

She couldn't help asking him why.

'You seem very dissimilar types.'

'You hardly know me,' she heard herself say, 'and you've known Decima little more than six weeks, I understand.'

'I see I've expressed myself badly,' he said. 'Let me put it this way: I've seen enough of Decima to enable me to form an opinion of her, and it wouldn't take five minutes' conversation with you to determine that you could never in a thousand years be placed in the category in which I should place Decima.'

'And what category is that? Or aren't I supposed to ask?'

'It would be better if you didn't, certainly. If I told you, you might feel bound to tell Decima as she's such a close friend.'

'And as you seem to think this would be a bad thing,' said Rachel, 'I assume your opinion of her can't be very high.'

'I didn't intend to imply that. Decima is very beautiful and very charming and an admirable hostess. I don't think anyone would quarrel with that.'

'No, indeed . . . She must have caused quite a stir in Oxford circles after she married Charles.'

'Yes, I believe she did. I'd left Oxford by that time so I never met her, although I continued to keep in touch with Charles after I left.' He was watching the St Bernard paddling at the water's edge. 'You knew Charles before he married Decima, I suppose?'

'Yes, Rohan introduced me to Charles when we – Rohan and I – were quite young. But we only saw him occasionally. He didn't come down to visit Rohan's family very often.'

'Charles is a remarkable man,' said Daniel, still watching the dog. 'Academically he's one of the most gifted men I've ever met.'

Rachel said nothing.

'Strange, isn't it,' said Daniel, 'how a very clever man should be quite so foolish?'

The waves crashed on the beach in a roar of surf, but she did not hear them.

'He should never have married Decima, of course. I'm only surprised he didn't see at the time how unsuited they were. Lord knows it must have been obvious enough.'

After a moment Rachel said: 'He – regrets the marriage?'

'Didn't Decima tell you their marriage was a mere formality?'

'Yes, but –'

'That was the main reason why my sister and I have stayed so long – the Mannerings begged us not to leave! They were both so bored with each other's company that they welcomed us with open arms. Didn't Decima tell you that? I'm sorry if I've said too much but I was under the impression you were in her confidence.'

It was only then that she realized he was trying to discover how much she knew and why she had come to Ruthven.

'There's been so little time,' she said, suddenly confused. 'Decima's hardly touched on the subject of either why you were here or why you had stayed so long.'

'Well, it's easy enough to explain.' He gestured towards a

flat slab of rock near the cliffs. 'Shall we sit down for a moment? Rebecca and I had decided to visit the Edinburgh Festival together – she'd just taken her postgraduate Diploma of Education exams and had planned to have a long holiday before looking around for a job, and my time is my own during the long vacation. Remembering that Charles had written to tell me of Ruthven during the years we had corresponded, I thought it might be interesting to hire a car after the Festival and drive up to the Highlands and over to the west coast. I wrote to Charles, telling him of the plans, and he wrote back by return mail to ask us to stay.

'I was intrigued by this place as soon as I saw it. I suppose every civilized man dreams from time to time of finding somewhere completely isolated and free from all the trappings of city and suburban life, but most of the time he never comes within a thousand miles of such a place. But Ruthven for me was the place of my dreams.' He stooped to run his index finger softly down the back of the dog at his feet. The wind from the sea flicked unseen fingers through his dark hair. 'But something happens to people,' he said after a while. 'Something happens to them when they're imprisoned between the mountains and the sea, cut off from other human beings and forced through necessity and circumstance to have much more contact with each other than would otherwise be the case. One finds oneself being sucked into a vortex; personality grates on personality in an ever-shifting pattern; everyone gets to know everyone else much too well for comfort.

'Rebecca and I should have left long ago, but we did not. For one thing Decima begged us to stay for her birthday, and for another . . . well, Charles too was anxious that we should stay, and I suppose the wish to leave wasn't strong enough.' He stopped. There was a pause. Then:

'I don't quite understand your remarks about a vortex,' Rachel said slowly. 'But surely Rohan's arrival – and now mine – must have eased matters if things were getting strained.'

'It would have been better if Quist had never set foot in this place,' said Daniel abruptly. 'And as for you . . . I can only advise you to leave as soon as you can. There are things going on here which I couldn't even begin to explain to you. Leave before you too get drawn into the vortex and find yourself unable to escape.'

Spray flew from the crashing surf. The tide was creeping farther towards them and from the south she could hear the roar of the undertow sucking over Cluny Sands.

'I don't understand you,' she said woodenly. 'What are you trying to say?'

A voice sounded above the roar of the surf. As they both swung round abruptly they saw Rebecca Carey walking towards them and, when she saw that they had noticed her, she raised her hand in greeting.

'But for God's sake,' said Daniel to Rachel, 'don't go repeating what I've said to Charles or Decima or Quist. I spoke for you and you alone.'

'Of course,' she said sharply, annoyed that he even considered it necessary to give her such a warning, and then she realized that her mouth was dry and her limbs stiff with tension.

Rebecca was already within earshot.

'This is the best morning we've had for days,' she called out, as she came up to them. 'You've brought good weather with you, Rachel.' The wind blew her short hair into her eyes, and she pushed it back impatiently. She wore a tweed skirt and an olive-green sweater, and the plain clothes were the perfect foil for the strong lines of her face and the glow of her eyes. It was a good-looking face, neither pretty nor beautiful, but Rachel thought her good looks were marred by a trace of aggression which seemed to hint that Rebecca had been accustomed all her life to reach out to grasp things she wanted, as they never came to her of their own accord. Rachel, who had gone to a large girls' day school before being exported to Geneva, had met a great many girls during her life and had no difficulty at all in placing Rebecca in the appropriate category. Rebecca was the one who sat in the front of the class and always knew all the answers, the girl whose tongue was as sharp as her brain and made enemies as fast as she tried to make friends, a lonely person in spite of her militant air of self-sufficiency.

With Rachel pity always outweighed dislike.

53

'You're up early,' she said pleasantly to Rebecca. 'Do you always go for a walk before breakfast?'

'I certainly don't wallow around in bed till ten with a breakfast tray, if that's what you mean. Danny, Charles is talking of going into Kyle of Lochalsh this morning to arrange for food for the dinner party. Didn't you say you wanted to go into town before Saturday evening to get Decima a present?'

'I'd thought of it.' He turned to Rachel. 'Do you have a present for Decima?'

'Yes, I've brought a small present up from London.'

'In that case, since you've had the experience of choosing a present for her, perhaps you'd care to come with us into town and help me select something? I've no idea what to buy for her and I'd appreciate some advice.'

'It will hardly be as difficult to choose as all that,' Rebecca said sharply before Rachel could reply. 'And I don't suppose Rachel wants to go back into Kyle of Lochalsh today.'

'I – I'm sure Rebecca could advise you just as well, Daniel—'

'As you wish.' He turned abruptly and set off at a brisk pace across the sands, the St Bernard padding in his wake.

'You'll probably find some very good Gaelic jewellery in town,' Rachel heard herself say in an instinctive attempt to gloss over the moment of awkwardness. 'It shouldn't be too difficult to find something suitable.'

'Exactly what I thought,' said Rebecca crisply. 'I'm surprised he asked you to come. He should have realized you would be too tired after your journey to want to do much today. How are you feeling, by the way? You look tired.'

'I—'

'As you're up so early, I suppose you didn't sleep well?'

'Well, actually, I—'

'It's always difficult getting used to a strange place, isn't it? And Ruthven must seem so primitive after the London suburbs ... Tell me, how did you come to meet Daniel this morning? I was looking for him everywhere.'

Rachel wondered for a fleeting moment why she always felt so irritated with people who prefaced all their questions with the words, 'Tell me.'

'I just met him down here on the beach,' she said shortly, and noticed in surprise that her feeling of irritation was growing with every second that passed; she very seldom allowed herself to be ruffled by a person's manner, but Rebecca seemed to have the most unfortunate effect on her.

'But why did you walk so far south? Cluny Sands—'

'Yes,' said Rachel politely. 'I've heard all about Cluny Sands.'

'You have? That's just as well ... They remind me of that novel by Sir Walter Scott – which was the one where the hero had trouble with quicksands? *Bride of Lammermoor*, was it? Or *Redgauntlet*? But of course, those quicksands were by the Firth of Forth.'

'Of course,' said Rachel, who had never read either novel. 'So they were.'

'You read Scott? Charles has a complete collection. What a wonderful library he has! It seems such a pity that Decima never reads anything except those ghastly women's magazines ... But then I believe she only had a very superficial education.'

'I expect she finds it adequate enough.'

'You think so? But then she's not really too clever, is she? And, of course, she's not too well either, I'm convinced of it.'

The cool hard drift of the conversation was suddenly crystallized into the ice of innuendo.

'What do you mean?' said Rachel sharply. 'Decima's as well as you or I!'

'Oh, but you haven't been living here these past few weeks as I have! She's really been acting in such a strange way – that's why we all encouraged her to have you to stay. Charles especially thought you would be good for her, a stabilizing influence ... She was getting rather – well, rather neurotic, although I hate to use a word with such unfortunate connotations. She's been giving poor Charles such a very difficult time.'

'I don't quite –'

'I can say all this to you, you see, because I really feel you should know the truth of the situation in order to be able to cope with Decima as you think best ... Ah, there's Ruthven! How fast Daniel's been walking! He's nearly by the jetty already ... And there's Rohan in the doorway – look, he's waving

55

to you! What a strange man he is, so foreign, so unusual. Tell me, he's not entirely English, is he?'

'His father came from Sweden. But about Decima—'

'Sweden? Oh well, of course, everyone knows the Swedes are a very strange race . . . Yes, it's really a great pity about Decima. I've made countless efforts to be sociable and friendly towards her, but she simply refuses to make any effort at all. Ever since we came here she's been hostile and trying to make things difficult for Charles – it's really been a constant source of embarrassment.'

'I'm surprised you stayed so long, then,' said Rachel, 'if you were unpopular with your hostess.'

'But my dear, there was no reason for her attitude! It was quite without motivation! Charles has confided to me once or twice that Decima is convinced that she's being persecuted in some way or another . . . As soon as they go back to Oxford he's arranging for her to see a doctor – you understand? I mean, it's not normal, is it? All she wants to do is hide from the world here in the back of beyond – she doesn't even want to go back to Oxford. Imagine not wanting to see Oxford again! I think she's afraid of meeting people, of showing herself. It's quite a common nervous complaint, I believe.'

'Decima seems eminently sane to me,' said Rachel, 'and I also disagree with your earlier remark about her intelligence. She was very clever indeed at school. Just because she's not intellectual doesn't mean to say she's not clever.'

'Well, of course,' said Rebecca, exactly as if Rachel hadn't spoken, 'the longer you stay here, the more apparent her state of mind will become to you. All I can say is that she's been acting very strangely lately.'

There was a small uncomfortable silence. Then:

'Rohan seems to want to talk to you,' Rebecca said as they watched him reach the beach and again wave to attract their attention. 'Will you excuse me? I want to find out what time Daniel plans to go into Kyle of Lochalsh.' And she was gone, her footsteps quickening across the sands.

Daniel was aboard the boat moored to the jetty, and as Rachel watched he came up from below deck and waited by the wheelhouse as he saw his sister coming. He seemed far away and remote, a minute part of the vast landscape of sea, sky and mountains.

'Ah, *there* you are!' said Rohan, stating what must have been obvious to him for at least five minutes. 'What's the matter with you, getting up so early?' He was still some way away from her, but his voice carried clearly on the still morning air. 'And why the secret rendezvous with Daniel?' he added as he came closer. 'I saw him follow you out of the house and across the sands! Rebecca looked most insulted when she came outside later and saw her beloved brother had walked off without her – usually they go together for their early morning stroll. What did Carey say to you anyway? What did he want?'

'It was nothing,' said Rachel automatically, her thoughts still on her conversation with Rebecca, and then as she thought of Daniel, she added a shade too positively, 'Absolutely nothing at all.'

'Ah-*ha*!' said Rohan at once. 'Ah-ha! My dear girl, don't tell me you find Carey irresistibly attractive! Don't tell me—'

'No, of course I shan't tell you, because it isn't true! Shut up, Rohan, for God's sake. It's too early in the morning for such nonsense . . . Listen, I want to talk to you – let's sit down here for a moment before we go on up to the house.'

'All right,' said Rohan agreeably, moving over to a long rock and subsiding on to it without argument. 'What's the matter? Did Carey—'

'Forget Daniel for a moment, would you? I want to talk about Rebecca.'

'Really? Do we have to? All right, all right, all right! Don't get huffy and walk off with your nose in the air! I was only joking. What's all this about Rebecca?'

'We've just had the most extraordinary conversation. She was saying such fantastic things that I was quite speechless.'

'Such as?'

'That – that Decima had a persecution complex—'

'Oh God!'

'– and was mentally ill—'

'What did you say?'

57

'What do you think I said? I told her as politely as possible that I thought she was the one who needed the psychiatrist, not Decima.'

'You didn't!'

'Well, no, to be honest, but I did deny it and say that Decima was as sane as we were.'

'Hm.'

'Well, isn't she? Don't be silly, Rohan! Look, what's been going on? Why should Rebecca say a thing like that? What happened here before I arrived yesterday?'

Rohan was silent. As she watched him she saw the amused lines about his mouth smooth themselves away and his grey eyes seemed to darken with his change of mood. 'There are several reasons why Rebecca should say a thing like that,' he said at last. 'First of all, Decima dislikes Rebecca and makes no effort to hide it. Secondly, Rebecca dislikes Decima for a good many reasons, the first and foremost of which is probably because Rebecca would always despise a woman less intellectual than herself. And thirdly, Decima really has been behaving very oddly.'

'I hadn't noticed. She seemed very normal to me.'

'Well, yes, naturally,' said Rohan. 'She was most successful at creating an atmosphere of normalcy when you arrived last night.'

After a moment Rachel said, 'I don't understand.'

'Things have been very far from normal, Rachel, and it all stems from Decima. I wouldn't say this to you if I hadn't known you all my life, because I know you and she were close friends for a while and as far as you're concerned you're still friends even though perhaps not such close friends as you were once. But I know you too damn well, Rachel, for insincerities, and I would be insincere if I didn't tell you that Decima's the last person who should ever be a friend of yours.'

'But I thought you liked Decima! When you first met her—'

'I didn't know her then, just as you don't know her now, but she's no good, Rachel. She's given Charles one hell of a time and I can tell you here and now he's at his wits' end with her. I keep telling him to divorce her, but they haven't been married three years yet, and it's not easy to get a divorce before then. Besides, he's against a divorce purely from a social point of view; divorce today hasn't the stigma it used to have, but he moves among elderly circles governed by a strict morality, and a divorce would certainly do him no good. However, it must obviously come to that in the end. I don't think she'll leave Ruthven to return to Oxford with him this time when term begins, and that'll mean a public acknowledgement of the rift between them.'

'He'll miss Decima's money if they're divorced, won't he?'

'Charles has enough money! He doesn't have to worry about that!'

'Nobody ever has enough money,' said Rachel ironically. 'No matter how much you have, it's never quite enough.'

'But Charles didn't marry Decima for her money, Rachel! He married her because he was infatuated with her looks, personality, sex-appeal – call it whatever you like! Perhaps you didn't see much of him before they were married and while they were engaged, but he was up to his eyes in his infatuation – and when a man's in love with a bank account instead of a pretty woman he hardly goes around with a moonstruck look in his eyes, unable to eat or sleep.'

'But when did the disillusionment begin? Wasn't it when he found she wouldn't consent to Ruthven's sale?'

'Is that what she says? Didn't she tell you anything about her marriage?'

'She mentioned that she'd been unhappy.'

'*She'd* been unhappy! My God! What about Charles? I don't know why she married him, but it certainly wasn't for love. Maybe she was attracted by the fact that he was an older man and a well-known name in academic life. Or maybe she was impressed by his charm and found the idea of marriage appealing. But she didn't love him! She may be beautiful and exotic and seductive but she's as cold as that northern sea out there, as empty and sterile as these desolate mountains around us. As far as any form of physical intimacy is concerned, she simply isn't interested. Whose idea was it, do you think, that they should have separate bedrooms? Certainly not Charles'!

Charles is a man, just like any other, when it comes to sex. He would even like children now, I think. But is Decima interested in children? Of course not! She doesn't care about anything except herself. Charles was a novelty to begin with, but she was soon bored. She yawned at the social occasions she had to attend with him, embarrassed him by her extravagances, humiliated him by making no attempt to fit into his world. She even flirted with the undergraduates in an effort to annoy him – but then she'd flirt with any man! Decima thrives on admiration.'

There was a long moment of silence. Then:

'There are two sides to everything,' said Rachel slowly at last, 'so I'm not surprised to hear there are two sides when it comes to the Mannerings' marriage. But here there are such wide discrepancies that one or the other party must be lying! According to Decima—'

'Yes, what on earth's Decima been saying? I didn't realize you'd already had the chance to speak to her.'

'We talked for a little while after dinner last night, and she implied she wasn't happy and that Charles had married her for her money. She also said that *he* had been acting strangely, and that—'

'Charles? But that's nonsense!'

'Is it? Anyway, she said she was glad I had come because I would act as a diversion by keeping *you* occupied. Then Charles wouldn't go on suspecting that you and Decima were having an affair.'

Rohan was suddenly white. 'Decima and I – but that's preposterous! Ridiculous! Absurd!' He stared at her, his grey eyes wide and dark, and for the first time since her arrival she saw through the mask of his light-hearted manner to the tension and fear which lay beneath. So Rohan too had somehow been drawn into the vortex which existed at Ruthven. Daniel's warning of the vortex rang once more in her ears, but before she could speak again Rohan was saying in a tight, controlled voice which she scarcely recognized: 'Decima was lying to you. Why should Charles suspect me of trying to have an affair with her when it's perfectly obvious that she's much more interested in Daniel Carey?'

60

CHAPTER FOUR

I

Daniel was watching Rohan and Rachel from the wheelhouse of the boat. They had been sitting on the rock together for ten minutes and still appeared to be deep in conversation.

'I don't like that girl,' Rebecca said from beside him.

'So I observed.' He lit a cigarette and the flame of the match was reflected for a moment in his eyes. He was thinking of Quist, wondering what game the man was playing, what he was saying to Rachel Lord a hundred yards away across the beach.

'Why on earth did you ask her to help you choose a present for Decima?'

He felt annoyed suddenly. 'Why not?' he said, wishing she would go back to the house and leave him alone for a while with his thoughts. 'I like her.'

'I wouldn't have thought she was your type.'

'Then I must be tired of my type – whatever that may be.' He went out on deck, but she followed him. He was reminded suddenly of the times when they had been children and Rebecca had always followed him faithfully wherever they had gone. It occurred to him vaguely that he was becoming a little tired of this childhood echo shadowing him wherever he went.

'I'm going back to the house,' he said shortly.

'I'll come with you.'

They returned in silence, not speaking till they reached the hall. Then: 'I'll call for you when I'm ready to leave,' he said over his shoulder and moved swiftly up the stairs to his room. On reaching the door he flung it shut behind him thankfully and did not at first notice that someone was waiting for him in the chair by the fireplace.

'Danny—'

He swung round. She stood up, graceful and poised as ever, and the folds of her pale blue peignoir seemed to float for a second in the draught of movement. 'Danny, I had to see you—'

'There's nothing to say.'

But she wasn't as meek as Rebecca, not as willing to accept the finality of his retorts. 'Listen, Daniel, I've changed my mind—'

'Then you've changed it too late, Decima. I'm sorry.' She was very close to him now; he noticed how she took a deliberate step nearer to him so that he could see how thin her peignoir was and how much excitement lay just beneath the lace surface. 'Please, Danny,' she said and her blue eyes were misty. 'Please . . .' It was cleverly done, he thought. In her own way she was an artist. And much to his anger and disgust he felt his pulses quicken as he allowed himself to look at her for a long moment. He would have turned away but she put a hand on his arm and halted him. 'I've treated you badly, I know, Danny; it was wrong of me and I realize that now. But I was frightened, anxious, scared . . .' She paused, searching his face for some glimmer of capitulation.

'You were none of those things,' he heard himself say. 'You were amused, flattered and diverted. Diverted because my attention provided a variation from the normal course of events at Ruthven, flattered because any woman likes being paid the kind of attention that I paid you, and amused because you're too cold to find anything except amusement in your power to interest a man when you yourself feel nothing at all.'

'That's not true!' she stormed, passionate and tempestuous now as if in a full demonstration of her emotional range. 'Just because I said no, just because I allowed myself one instant of loyalty to Charles, just because for a moment I was frightened by the depth of my feelings for you—'

'You didn't care, Decima, and no matter how hard you try now to play the role of the loyal young wife beset with temptations, you'll never make the part convincing. You refused because you didn't care, and once I realized that and saw your masquerade for what it was, I didn't care either.'

'But I do care, I do! I'll do whatever you want, Danny, I swear it – just say what you want me to do and I'll do it!'

'You don't understand,' he said coldly as the hot sweat moistened the palms of his hands. 'You're making the situation much more complex than it really is. The position was simply this: I saw you, wanted you, just as I'd want any other attractive woman. After you'd played around and successfully kept me at arm's length while you amused yourself watching my growing frustration, it eventually dawned on me that you were never going to be interested enough to say yes and, even if you did, you probably wouldn't have much to offer in the end. I'm not interested in cold women. And as soon as I lost interest in you sexually, I'm afraid that was the end of your power over me. Next time I'd advise you to play your cards a little differently if you want your fun to last longer.'

She was very white. For a moment he had the unnerving impression that he had misjudged her and that she was, after all, capable of caring, and so strong was the impression that he instinctively drew closer to her.

The next thing he knew was that she was in his arms and her mouth was beneath his own.

Her lips were very far from being cold.

After a long moment she said, 'Take me away from Charles.'

He looked at her. It did not seem preposterous at all, merely the most natural thing in the world. He was still looking at her when there was a soft knock at the door and they both spun round.

'Daniel?' called Charles softly. 'May I come in?'

II

Daniel took several seconds to answer the door. It vaguely occurred to Charles to wonder why he was taking so long and then, before he could question it further, the door was opening and Daniel was on the threshold.

'I'm sorry, Charles, I wasn't sure whether I heard you ... Won't you come in?'

'No, I was only going to tell you that I plan to leave for Kyle of Lochalsh at ten-thirty – will that be convenient for you?'

'Fine. I'll tell Rebecca.'

'I've already told her,' said Charles, moving on down the corridor. 'I'll see you later, Daniel,' and he was gone.

Daniel closed the door just as Decima emerged from her hiding-place behind the long curtains.

'I keep thinking he suspects something,' she said. 'Supposing he knows. Or supposing he suspects—'

'How can he when there's nothing to suspect?' He had himself tightly in control now. He knew exactly which course he was going to take and exactly how he was going to manage the situation. It was as if the brief interval with Charles had sharpened his sensibilities and frozen the heat in his body to ice. 'There's nothing between us now, Decima, and as far as I'm concerned there never will be.'

'But just now—' Her eyes were brilliant with anger, her face white with fury. 'Just now—'

'Just now I was a fool, Decima, but I'm not such a fool as to make the same mistake twice. If you want to escape from your marriage, you must find someone else to help you, for the help won't be coming from me.'

She still stood looking at him. 'But why?' she said at last. 'Why? I thought a few days ago that you felt quite differently.'

'I'm sorry if I misled you,' he said, turning abruptly as if to terminate the conversation, 'but I'm afraid there's nothing more to be said.'

He waited for her to speak again, to demand a further explanation or even to lose her temper, but she was silent. And then very slowly she said: 'You're sure you won't regret that, aren't you?'

He swung round. Her face was still white but her mouth was smiling.

'Regret what?' His voice was cool and casual in his ears.

'You don't want to get a bad reputation in academic circles, do you?' she said, turning from him to open the door. 'They're really so fussy about professors nowadays, I've heard.'

And she was gone, closing the door lightly behind her and leaving him alone at last in the solitude of his room.

Decima was not in her room when Rachel called for breakfast at nine-thirty. The large light room was neat, the bed already made, and from the window Rachel had an uninterrupted view south-east to the moors and mountains and south-west to the sea. She was just wondering whether to seek Decima downstairs when the door opened and Decima herself came quickly into the room.

'Ah, there you are!' Her cheeks were flushed and her eyes very bright, as if she were very excited. Or very angry. 'I'll call for Mrs Willie to bring up the breakfast tray. Did you sleep well?'

'Fine, thanks. I awoke early and went for a walk along the beach ... Is anything the matter, Decima? You look a little uneasy.'

'No, it's nothing. Just nervousness ... I think we'll all be going into town this morning, by the way, so I hope you'll come with me and keep me company. Daniel and Rebecca have to do some personal shopping and I have to go with Charles to order the food for the dinner party. As there's been no shooting party I'm afraid we'll have to buy the venison. You wouldn't mind coming, would you?'

'Not in the least. It's a beautiful morning for a boat trip ... What time is Charles planning to go?'

'About ten-thirty – if I can be ready by then. I'm so bad at getting up in the mornings.'

This turned out to be perfectly true. In the end it was after eleven o'clock by the time everyone was aboard the boat and Charles was starting up the motor.

The sun was pleasantly warm; Rachel, sitting near the stern with the soft wind caressing her skin, found it hard in the light of day to recall her fears of the previous evening after dark or even her fears of that same morning during her conversation with Daniel by Cluny Sands. Everyone seemed perfectly normal. Charles and Rohan were in the wheelhouse, Decima was beside her on the seat and the Careys were in the prow of the boat, near enough to talk to each other but each appearing to maintain silence. She watched the back of Daniel's head and then Rohan came out of the wheelhouse to join them and she glanced out to sea abruptly.

'Are you all right, Decima? You look a little chilled.'

'No, I'm fine.'

Something was definitely wrong with Decima. Rohan and Rebecca had been right after all. Glancing at her friend, Rachel noticed the nervous workings of her fingers on the material of her skirt, the restlessness of her eyes, the tenseness in every line of her slim body. She had had nothing for breakfast except a cup of coffee, and had talked rapidly in fits and starts of any random topic which came to her mind. It had been an uncomfortable meal and Rachel had been glad when it was over.

Rebecca was moving. As Rachel watched, she left Daniel in the prow and went into the wheelhouse for a word with Charles before slipping below decks and out of sight.

Rachel began to watch Daniel again.

'Let's go below,' Rohan was saying. 'I'll make you some coffee, Decima.'

'No, thanks.'

'Sure? How about you, Rachel?'

'What?'

'Would you like some coffee?'

'Oh . . . no thanks, Rohan.' Daniel had turned around and was coming towards them. The breeze was suddenly icy-cool against her hot cheeks.

'Wait, Rohan,' said Decima clearly. 'I think I will come below with you.'

'You will? Fine. Sure you won't change your mind, Raye?'

She hardly heard him. Daniel was smiling at her, sitting down in the seat which Decima had just left. 'I'm sorry I was rather abrupt with you this morning,' he was saying. 'I'm afraid I left you very suddenly with my sister.'

He was sitting next to her in a casual, relaxed position, his legs stretched out and crossed at the ankles, one elbow on the back of the seat to ease the pressure on his spine so that his body was turned slightly towards her. She felt stiff and awkward suddenly, wanting to relax and yet afraid of betraying her taut muscles by one careless movement, wanting to look at him, yet not trusting herself to meet his eyes. Her awareness of him was so immense that she thought that even if he had held her in his arms it would have been impossible for her to have felt more at the mercy of her own emotions. And for Rachel, who had always prided herself on the level-headed advice she had given, when requested, to her love-lorn friends, such a complete reversal of her self-possession seemed to strip her of all vestiges of confidence.

She looked at him suddenly, determined that he should never know the effect he had on her, and said with candour, 'Decima doesn't seem herself at all this morning. I was wondering what was the matter with her, but she says nothing is wrong.'

He shrugged. 'She's easily upset, it seems . . . How calm the sea is today! The landscape looks almost at peace. Have you been to Scotland before, by the way, or is this your first visit?'

She answered him readily enough, but she had noticed how deftly he had avoided a discussion of Decima. He asked her more questions about her life in London, even about her recent visit to Florence and, while she answered, she was wondering if he had had an affair with Decima and abused Charles' hospitality in the most shameful of all ways possible. Yet Rohan had not said positively that Daniel and Decima were having an affair, only that Decima was much too interested in her guest . . . And Decima had said the previous evening that she disliked Daniel Carey and that she didn't trust him.

Either Rohan was mistaken, thought Rachel, or Decima was lying. Probably Decima was lying because she wanted Rachel's support against Charles and feared Rachel might disapprove of a confession of infidelity; she wouldn't have wanted to risk losing Rachel's sympathy at that particular moment.

Probably, too, they were having an affair. She doubted very much whether Decima would be cold and remote if she were strongly attracted to a man, and surely Daniel would have left Ruthven days ago if he had failed from the outset to get what he wanted. A man like Daniel Carey would probably always get what he wanted from women with very little trouble.

'I often go down to London from Cambridge for a weekend,' he was saying. 'We must arrange to meet some time. Did you say you enjoyed the theatre?'

And then she was lost again, lost to the cool clear voice of her reason appraising the situation, lost to all her sensible powers of judgement. Yes, she loved the theatre, she went as often as possible, as often as she could afford it . . .

'Afford it?' said Daniel, his fine eyes alive with surprise. 'Are your escorts so mean they allow you to pay your own way?'

Normally she would have been too proud to admit that she seldom had the opportunity of an escorted visit to the theatre, but some strange instinct made her be honest with him just when she most wanted to be dishonest.

'It's only girls like Decima who have a string of escorts lining up to take them out every night of the week!' she said lightly. 'The rest of us aren't so fortunate. If I had to wait for a generous escort every time I wanted to see a play I wouldn't go to the theatre nearly as often as I like.'

He was so astonished that she almost laughed. 'You mean you go on your own?'

'Yes, of course – why not? Or perhaps I may go with a girl friend. But I don't sit around at home like a modern Cinderella if I haven't got someone to take me out.'

He stared at her.

This time she did laugh. 'You look as if I've just destroyed all your conventional ideas about young single women!'

He laughed too. 'No. it's hardly as drastic as that, but nonetheless . . .' He glanced away, and she did not at first realize that he was checking that no one else was within earshot. 'Nonetheless, it confirms my original impression of you.'

'And what was that?'

'That you're a most unusual and interesting woman.' He was on his feet, not looking at her, and the breeze tore at his dark hair for a moment as he stepped over to the wheelhouse.

'May I borrow a cigarette from you, Charles? I seem to have used my last one . . . Thanks.'

She was watching him, noticing every movement, her mind

68

teeming with every echo of their conversation and recalling every inflection of his voice. Charles gave him a cigarette and he paused in the shelter of the wheelhouse to light it. And then, before he could return to her, Rebecca emerged from below decks and the chance to renew the conversation was gone.

Rachel turned away and stared across the sea at the inland mountains.

It was after one when they reached Kyle of Lochalsh. After they had found a place for the boat in the harbour, Charles suggested they have lunch before doing anything further, but Daniel had little enthusiasm for the idea and in the end he and Rebecca separated from the others and walked off into the town on their own. Daniel again asked Rachel to come with them, but Decima at once said that Rachel had agreed to help her buy food for the dinner-party. Daniel had shrugged and said nothing further.

It was curious, Rachel thought, how everyone seemed to relax once the Careys had gone. Charles became more jovial, Rohan more loquacious and Decima less painfully ill at ease. Rachel could even feel her own tenseness evaporate once Daniel had gone, but her thoughts were still in such turmoil that it was hard for her to concentrate afresh on Decima's troubles and the situation surrounding her. Making a great effort, she managed to answer the remarks that were addressed to her, but all the time she was thinking of Daniel and remembering how he had already suggested travelling from Cambridge to London to see her.

And suddenly she didn't care what his relationship with Decima was or had been, didn't even care whether in fact it had ever existed. With something of a shock she realized she didn't care about Decima any more either. In a moment of honesty with herself she saw vividly that her world had assumed new and frightening dimensions; it was as if quite without warning she had been swept off her feet by a strong current, borne turbulently along on the crest of a huge, silent tide over which she had no control. *I'm no longer an outsider looking in at the scene being played before me*, she thought, *but part of the scene itself.*

And she felt not only a strange sense of exuberance but also a sharp pang of dread.

She had been drawn into the vortex.

IV

Daniel said to his sister: 'Things are getting dangerous.'

'With Decima?'

'The situation's getting out of hand. I was a fool ever to get involved with her.'

Rebecca was shocked. Daniel never made a fool of himself over a woman. 'What do you mean, Danny? Why do you say that?'

He told her. They were walking up the High Street past the shops selling tweeds and tartans, past the butcher, the baker, the greengrocer, but by the time they reached the little shop selling Gaelic silverware and jewellery, Rebecca had long since ceased to be conscious of her surroundings.

'My God, Danny—'

'So you can see how dangerous it is.'

'But she'll have to be stopped! Something will have to be done!'

'That's my worry, not yours.'

'But of course it's my worry too! She could ruin you, Danny – do you think I would stand by and see that happen? How can you say it's not my worry?'

'You've problems of your own without involving yourself in mine.'

'But I'm already involved! Danny, the associate professorship you were hoping to get – supposing Decima should—'

'Precisely.'

'But what shall we do?'

'You will do nothing at all,' said Daniel quietly, 'what I shall do remains to be seen.'

V

They had bought all that was necessary for the dinner-party after lunching at one of the inns near the harbour; Rachel had gone with Decima to buy the venison and the rest of the food while Rohan had gone with Charles to attend to buying the champagne and an assortment of other bottles that were considered necessary. By the time all the purchases were safely on board it was after three-thirty and there was still no sign of the Careys.

'I think I'll stroll over to the pub at the jetty, and coax the landlord to serve me a pint of beer outside licensing hours,' said Rohan. 'Then I'll see the Careys when they arrive back at the boat. Will anyone come with me?'

'Perhaps I will,' Charles said. 'Decima?'

'No, I'm too tired. I'll wait here.'

'I'll stay with Decima,' said Rachel, before she could be asked. 'You two go off and have your beer.'

When they had gone Decima complained of a headache and went aft to make herself coffee in the tiny galley. 'Do you want some, Raye?'

'No, thanks. I'm going up on deck, I think. Will you be all right down here?'

'Yes, I'll have some coffee and then lie down for a minute. I hope the Careys won't be too long. I feel like going home now.'

'I'll give you a call when I see them.' She went up on the deck and moved into the wheelhouse to escape the increasing chill of the sea breeze. It was cloudier now, the best part of the day already over, and the sea was swaying restlessly as if in anticipation of rain to come.

She began to wonder where Daniel was and what he was doing.

She had scarcely been five minutes in the wheelhouse before she saw him. He was walking towards the jetty with Rebecca, and as they passed the pub Rohan and Charles must have attracted their attention, for they stopped and looked at one of

71

the downstairs windows. Presently Rebecca went inside the pub, but Daniel remained outside and as Rachel watched he started walking away from the building towards the jetty and the boat.

There was a tightness suddenly beneath her heart, a hollow in the pit of her stomach. She sat perfectly still, watching him walk the length of the jetty, and as she watched it seemed to her that she had been waiting for many years without knowing what she was waiting for, knowing only that she would recognize the moment when it came.

He reached the boat, saw her, smiled. The hull shifted in the water as he climbed aboard.

'I thought I'd find you here,' he said. 'Where's Decima?'

'Down in the cabin, resting.'

'I see.' He stepped into the wheelhouse beside her and glanced down the jetty towards the pub but no one was in sight. 'The others should be here in a minute.'

'Yes, I saw Rebecca go in to fetch them.'

There was a silence.

Rachel was steadfastly watching the grey stone walls of the pub with its swaying sign above the doorway. Presently she felt Daniel's hand on her arm, and as she glanced round at him instinctively, he began to speak. 'Don't believe—' But he stopped.

The sentence was never completed.

Afterwards all Rachel could remember was the grip of his fingers on her wrists and the harsh warmth of his lips on her mouth. There was heat, a blaze of power, the pressure of hard muscles taut in a hard, strong body, and then suddenly it was over and the dark dizziness was ebbing before her eyes so that she could see at last past Daniel to the deck where Decima stood frozen in immobility as she watched them.

Rachel felt her lips move.

Daniel spun round.

'Well, well,' said Decima politely in her softest, sweetest voice. 'It seems as if I underestimated you, Raye. You certainly don't waste much time, do you? So sorry to interrupt you both at such a terribly awkward moment but I thought I'd just tell you that the others have left the pub and are on their way over here ...'

VI

It was raining by the time they reached Ruthven. Heavy clouds had sunk over the mountain summits and laid dark fingers across the moors behind the sands. After making her escape as quickly as possible to her room, Rachel found that the fire was already lit and the housekeeper had just put a ewer of hot water on the washstand for her.

She undressed thankfully, stripping off the clothes which had become sodden in the short journey from the jetty to the house, and huddled herself in the quilt from the bed for a moment before taking advantage of the warm water.

She was just putting on her wool dress some minutes later when there was a soft tap at the door.

'Who's that?'

'Decima.'

Oh God, thought Rachel. She could already feel the crimson of embarrassment suffusing her neck and creeping upwards to her face. Decima was the last person she wanted to talk to.

'I'm just dressing for dinner, Decima – can it wait?'

'No, I want to talk to you.'

The zip fastener at the side of the dress jammed in her hot fingers. 'Just a moment.'

The zip refused to go either up or down. 'Oh hell!' muttered Rachel at last, abandoning it, and wrenched open the door much more violently than she had intended.

Decima was dressed for dinner. She wore black, a plain, simple dress, and above her left breast was a diamond brooch which glittered in the dim glow of the lamp and firelight.

'Yes?' said Rachel abruptly.

Decima moved into the room without speaking. Then as Rachel closed the door: 'I just wanted to warn you about Daniel.'

Rachel suddenly felt very angry indeed. After all, what right did Decima have to enable her to act so possessively where Daniel was concerned? Decima a married woman, had much less right to Daniel than she had and certainly no right at all to criticize Rachel's behaviour with him. 'I've nothing to say about Daniel,' she heard herself say coolly. 'I'm only surprised that you should want to talk about him.'

Decima raised her eyebrows slightly. 'You're very quick to take offence all of a sudden, aren't you? Why should you feel so guilty just because I saw you kissing Daniel this afternoon at Kyle of Lochalsh? Is a kiss such a novel experience for you that you're overcome with remorse and shame for days afterwards?'

'I—'

'I only wanted to warn you that Daniel has a very accomplished way with women. Charles tells me that when Daniel was an undergraduate at Oxford—'

'I'm not interested,' said Rachel furiously, 'in past gossip. I don't care how many affairs Daniel has had and, even if I did care, it's certainly none of my business. But what I *am* interested in is why you deliberately misled me last night when you came here to tell me about Charles! Why did you lie and say that Daniel wasn't interested in women and that you didn't trust him when you'd been secretly having an affair with him for the past few weeks?'

The light was uncertain but she thought she saw Decima turn very pale. 'I – I was too ashamed . . . I thought if I could avoid telling you—'

'How much else have you avoided telling me, Decima?'

There was a long, still silence. 'What do you mean?'

'I couldn't help wondering how much the failure of your marriage was Charles' fault and how much was yours.'

Another silence. Then, 'I—' she hesitated. 'I suppose we were both to blame in some ways . . . I was so angry when I saw Charles had married me for my money that I didn't behave very well at Oxford . . . There was nothing wrong, you understand, but once or twice I drank too much at the sedate cocktail parties, and embarrassed Charles. And I flirted now and again with a couple of students, just out of boredom . . . But I was never unfaithful! Even now, with Daniel, even though he begged me and begged me to be unfaithful to Charles, I always

74

somehow managed to keep my head and refuse him. Rachel, you've no idea what a strain I've had to endure these past few weeks! I was genuinely attracted to Daniel but was terrified in case Charles should find out. Then I began to wonder if Charles was secretly encouraging Daniel, so that once I was proved unfaithful he would have the excuse for any kind of revenge. I could hardly believe, you see, that Daniel would behave so shamefully to Charles, whom I knew he respected and liked.'

'That certainly seems hard to believe, but how much encouragement did you give him?'

'None at all, I swear it! But I find him attractive, I admit it, and sometimes it was very hard – in fact, impossible – to keep aloof from him. Perhaps it's hard for you to understand, but—'

Rachel found it all too easy to understand. She was beginning to feel slightly sick; her head ached dully. 'I'm surprised Charles didn't realize what was happening.'

'That's why I began to think he was secretly conniving at Daniel's behaviour. He even encouraged the Careys to stay at Ruthven as long as possible! And then I began to think – imagine – all kinds of things; I thought they might all be in a plot against me, manoeuvring me into some terrible position from which there was no retreat . . . I – I've been so frightened, Raye, it's all been such a nightmare . . .' She was trembling; she had to sit down. 'I'm sorry if I behaved badly to you this afternoon when I saw you with Daniel, but my nerves were in such shreds that I couldn't even think clearly. It just seemed to me that you, the only person I could trust, were being gradually prised away and turned against me, and the thought was so shattering and frightful that I lost control of myself altogether. You do believe me, don't you, Raye? You're not against me, are you?'

'Of course not,' said Rachel shortly. 'Don't be silly.' But beneath her reassuring manner, she was badly shaken; her mind a mass of conflicts and doubts.

It was undeniably true that everyone she had spoken to that day had tried to turn her against Decima. It was probably also true that Daniel was so accustomed to getting his own way with women that he couldn't resist amusing himself with her. No doubt he had thought her quaint and old-fashioned and had enjoyed seeing how much he could disconcert her and disrupt her conventional behaviour.

The headache had become a tight pain behind the eyes.

'Have you got some aspirin by any chance, Decima?'

'Aspirin? Yes, of course ... Listen, why don't we have dinner together in my room? I don't want to face the others again tonight. We could have a quiet dinner and talk for a while and then have an early night.'

'Wouldn't that look rather suspicious? Anyway, I'm well enough – it's just a slight headache. I really think I'd better dine with everyone else.'

In spite of everything, she still had no wish to miss an opportunity to see Daniel. As she returned from Decima's room with the aspirin bottle five minutes later she wondered how she could still find him attractive when she knew beyond any doubt that he could not care for her.

Daniel cared only for Decima; the entire scene in the wheel-house that afternoon had probably been enacted with the specific intent of making Decima jealous in the hope of increasing her interest in him.

Twenty minutes later, her headache eased, she went down to the dining-room for dinner.

Decima made no appearance at dinner, but Charles and Rohan were talkative enough and spent most of the meal discussing plans for the dinner-party on the following evening while recalling their own twenty-first birthday celebrations years earlier; in contrast, Rebecca said little and Rachel too found she had less than usual to say. Daniel did not look at her once throughout the entire meal and said no word to anyone. At the earliest opportunity he excused himself and withdrew from the room.

Rebecca at length went off to the library to read; Charles retired to his study to look at his manuscript for a while, and Rachel and Rohan were left facing each other across the table.

Rohan leant forward to move the candelabra. 'Why didn't Decima come down tonight?'

'She said she was tired.'

'And what do you say she was?'

'She certainly looked tired. She really is in a very nervous state, Rohan. I feel quite worried about her.'

'If her nerves are in a bad way,' said Rohan, 'she has only herself to blame.'

'Oh? And what's that remark supposed to mean?'

'She could leave tomorrow if she wanted to.'

'Don't be a fool! How could she possibly walk out on this celebration dinner-party which has been so carefully arranged and planned? She's committed to staying here at least until the morning of her birthday. And she tells me she hasn't the cash in hand to leave before then anyway.'

'You're attracted to Daniel, aren't you? No, don't try and tell me that's nonsense! I know you too well, Rachel – I know when you like a man and when you don't. But you can forget Daniel. He's totally absorbed in Decima.'

'I—' Rachel began, but Rohan wasn't listening.

'Do you think I didn't notice as soon as I came to Ruthven how things were between them?' he interrupted. 'Do you think it wasn't obvious to me that he wanted her and was trying every trick he knew to get her to go away with him?' His voice was a little unsteady. As if to cover up his lack of self-possession, he reached for the carafe of wine and clumsily poured some more into his glass. But his hand was trembling; the wine spilt into dark red pools on the white cloth. 'I told Charles,' he said. 'But he didn't believe me. Can you imagine that? This morning after I left you I saw Decima slip into Daniel's room to wait for him to come back from the boat, and I knew damn well what she was waiting for. I went to Charles and said—'

'You had no right to do that, Rohan. It's no concern of yours,' Rachel interrupted sharply.

'Charles is my cousin, isn't he?'

'That's got nothing to do with it. You had no right to interfere.'

'Christ Almighty!' shouted Rohan, setting down his glass with such a crash that the frail stem seemed to shiver. 'Don't preach to me! Don't get up into your little Victorian pulpit and preach sermons to me about what to do and what not to do! What do you know about life anyway? You've never been in love, never gone to bed with anyone, never—'

'What on earth's that got to do with you sneaking to Charles to tell him that his guest's trying to seduce his wife? Good God, if Charles hasn't the perception to see when a guest of his is behaving disgracefully, he deserves to have his wife seduced! I'm not surprised he didn't welcome you interfering in his affairs!'

'But if he knew Daniel was trying to seduce Decima, why the hell didn't he throw Daniel out of Ruthven? And besides, he didn't believe me when I told him about them! He was so vain, so incredibly pompous and conceited that he thought it was impossible that Decima should ever think of being unfaithful to him! And all along he's insisted that the Careys stay at Ruthven!'

'Then either he's a fool or else he has special reasons of his own for keeping the Careys here.'

'What reasons?' demanded Rohan. 'Give me one good reason why he should continue to keep his wife's lover in his house!'

'According to Decima, they're not lovers.'

'If they're not, it's not for want of trying on Daniel's part!'

'How do you know?'

He stared at her. 'I've been watching them.'

'Spying on them, you mean, don't you?'

'I—'

'For God's sake, Rohan, what on earth are you trying to do? Are you Charles' self-appointed private eye, or something? To be quite blunt, what is it to you whether Decima goes to bed with Daniel or not?'

Rohan pulled back his chair and stood up so abruptly that the chair fell over backwards. 'It's quite obvious,' he said, striding over to the door, 'that you haven't the slightest grasp of the situation at all.'

She allowed him thirty seconds for his rage to cool and then followed him into the little drawing-room off the great hall. He was standing by the blazing log fire, and in his hands was a carved ivory paper-knife which he had apparently picked up from the desk in his agitation. The ivory was curved like a tusk, and the upper half of the tusk was the sheath into which the blade of the knife could be inserted, while the lower half of the tusk was the handle in which the blade was embedded. Rachel could not remember seeing it before.

'Where did that come from?'

'It's Rebecca's. She bought it in Edinburgh just before she came to Ruthven.' He put it down abruptly, and she saw that the carvings on the ivory surface were of Chinese figures, each perfectly executed and designed.

She picked it up idly.

'There are two questions I should like to see answered,' said Rohan suddenly. 'First, why should Charles tolerate Daniel's behaviour and in fact actively encourage the Careys to stay, and second, why should Decima have chosen to stay here when she had the means and opportunity to escape earlier?'

'Ruthven *is* her home, Rohan. Why should she allow herself to be driven away?' She pulled the tusk apart absent-mindedly, and ran her index finger along the edge of the blade. 'Goodness, this knife's sharp! You could dissect an Aberdeen Angus with it.' She sucked her finger where a faint line of red was already showing, and put the knife back on the table.

'But surely,' Rohan was saying, 'if Decima was really in such a state of nerves as the result of her relationship with Daniel or Charles or both of them, would she care much about leaving Ruthven for a while? Wouldn't she be merely glad to escape?'

'But what chance has there been for her to escape?'

'Daniel—'

'I'm quite sure that Daniel wouldn't have been so foolish as to commit himself in that way.'

'How do you know?' said Rohan. 'He's little more than a stranger to you. How do you know what he might or might not do?'

The knife was a mere white blur on the polished surface of the table. Rachel picked it up again blindly, her fingers working over the cool surface. Everything Rohan said was true. What did she know of Daniel? How did she know that Daniel hadn't

79

asked Decima to go away with him and then, on her refusal, had paid Rachel attention to make Decima jealous? Wasn't it obvious that the scene in the wheelhouse had merely been to incite Decima to re-examine her feelings for him? It had clearly been a successful manoeuvre, for that same evening at Ruthven Decima had come to her to try to turn her against Daniel so that she might have him for herself once more.

Decima, with her money and beauty and her effortless, graceful poise . . . It was so easy to picture her with Daniel, much easier to picture her with him than with Charles. It seemed that Decima was playing some game of her own, planning all the time to go away with Daniel eventually.

'Is anything the matter, Rachel? You look very white.'

Decima had always had what she wanted. Life was very easy for people like Decima who were constantly beset with favours and attentions, admirations and compliments. Daniel would seem just like any other man to her, another name to add to the long list of men who had stopped to look at her more than once. Decima didn't need Daniel except to use him in obtaining whatever it was she wanted. Decima didn't care.

But Rachel cared. 'No,' she said. 'Nothing's the matter.'

'Has Daniel—'

'I don't want to talk about Daniel any more.' The knife slipped from her hands and fell loudly on the table. 'I think I'll go to bed early. My headache seems to be getting worse.'

'If you want some aspirin—'

'No, Decima gave me some already, thanks. Goodnight, Rohan.'

'Goodnight,' he said slowly, and she knew, even though she did not glance back at him, that his grey eyes were sharp and watchful as he noted her withdrawal and drew his own conclusions from her behaviour. Rohan always saw too much.

Moving swiftly, hardly knowing where she was going, she found her way across the hall and stumbled upstairs to the comforting privacy of her room.

VII

She awoke very suddenly just after midnight. The wind was whispering at the window again and humming in the eaves, and the rain was a light, stealthy patter against the pane. It was pitch dark. All she could see was the luminous dial of her little travelling clock and the white strip of the sheet turned down over the quilt.

She sat up listening.

The house was still, yet something had woken her. Maybe she had been dreaming and, on awakening, had confused the dream with consciousness.

She went on listening but heard nothing, and presently she slipped out of bed and moved across to the door without lighting the lamp. She was just about to ease the door open when she heard the creak of a floorboard in the corridor outside. Unreasonably, her scalp tingled. Her limbs froze, and movement was impossible. She was suddenly and uncontrollably frightened.

It was hard to judge how long she stood there in the darkness waiting, but after a minute of complete silence she managed to edge noiselessly back to her bedside table and find the matches to light the lamp. The glow of light was reassuring. With the lamp in her hand she turned back to the door. No doubt she was being foolish and would laugh at herself in the clear light of morning, but she knew she would be unable to fall asleep easily again unless the door was locked.

It was not until she reached the door that she discovered that there was no key in the lock.

Perhaps it was on the other side.

It was at least two minutes before she could bring herself to turn the handle and pull the door slowly inward towards herself. There was no one outside. Stepping into the corridor quickly, she saw it was empty.

There was still no sign of a key. She paused, uncertain of what she should do, and as she hesitated she saw that there was a faint glow at the far end of the corridor, as if a large lamp was still burning downstairs in the hall. Suddenly making up her

mind she blew out her lamp, leaving it in her room, and returned to the passage.

Decima's door, farther down on the right of the corridor, was
closed and, although Rachel knocked lightly on the panels and
called out softly to ask if she were asleep, there was no reply.
She tried the handle but the door was locked. Decima at least
had a key for her room.

Rachel moved on. The gallery when she reached it was in
darkness but, as she glanced over the banisters, she saw that
one of the large lamps was indeed burning on the table in the
hall below. Again she paused. Her knowledge of the house was
still slight, but she knew that her room was in the south wing
of the house and that Decima's room was in the south-east
turret with windows which overlooked both the mountains and
moors in the east and the sands and cliffs to the south. Charles
apparently had rooms in the west wing which faced the sea, and
she could remember Rohan mentioning that his room also
faced the ocean. The north wing was no longer used, the gamekeeper and his wife now preferring to live in the small croft a
hundred yards from the house. This meant that the Careys had
probably been given rooms in the east wing which faced the
mountains and moors, and it was in the east wing that Rachel
now stood. Unlike the other wings of the house, the corridor
was open on one side so that it was possible to look over the
banisters into the great hall below, and half-way down the
corridor the twin staircases linking the two floors curved to
meet in a wide landing. At the far end of the corridor, a more
insignificant staircase spiralled upwards in the north-east
turret to lead to empty rooms on higher, deserted floors, but
the main staircase, beginning as it did in the great hall itself,
had more style and elegance. On the side of the corridor which
did not face the hall and stairs, six doors led into the six rooms
of the east wing. As she moved towards the landing and the
head of the stairs, she saw that one of the doors was ajar.

She stopped.

The room was in darkness. After a moment's hesitation she
tapped the panels, but when no one responded she pushed the
door open wider and glanced into the room.

The bed was unslept in, the curtains of the windows still undrawn, but the embers of a fire burnt in the grate and from their glow there was sufficient light for her to see without the aid of a lamp.

Daniel kept his room neat. A pair of masculine slippers stood near the bed; a dressing-gown lay precisely across one of the high-backed armchairs where it had been placed, not thrown, by its owner. There was a pair of silver clothes-brushes on the high dresser, a large plain comb beside them, and by the washstand was an old-fashioned razor set incongruously beside a modern tube of shaving cream.

Not wanting to pry among his belongings she withdrew quickly to the corridor again, but not before she was aware of her curiosity to explore further, to strain to discover more about him than the facts she already knew. After the scene in the wheelhouse that afternoon, she was conscious of an immense desire to find other evidence of his personality, other clues of his past. How had his life been spent when he was away from his books and his research? What had his childhood been like, his adolescence? Had there been disappointments and disillusionment or had the path of his success been so clearly marked from the beginning that he had never known the pain of failure or the pangs of frustration? Had he many friends at Cambridge? Did he live alone there, or—

But she decided not to pursue this line of thought. She had already told Rohan in indignation that she was not concerned with Daniel's past relations with the opposite sex, and to dwell upon the subject now would make her earlier remark seem hypocritical.

Moving quickly as if to shake off all thought of Daniel's possible associations, she left the room and went out onto the landing again.

There was still no one in sight.

Then where was Daniel? And who had left the light burning in the hall?

It was not until she was halfway down the stairs that it occurred to her to wonder if Decima really had been sleeping so soundly behind her locked door. She stopped, her hand on the

83

banisters as she glanced back over her shoulder at the silent gallery she had just left.

It was then she heard the sound of voices. They seemed far away, a mere murmur sighing through the vast silence of the hall, but on reaching the last stair she found the sound was coming from one of the rooms leading off the hall to the left of the staircase. She stepped over to the library, and then realized that the voices came from Charles' study next door, the ground floor of the south-east turret.

She drew nearer. The door was almost shut and the occupants of the room obviously believed that it was completely closed; having been about to knock and enter to find out who was up so late, Rachel instinctively hesitated as the first snatches of conversation reached her ears.

'No,' Charles Mannering was saying strongly. 'That would be out of the question. My dear, you've attended University. You know how things are. Of course, if I were free it would be a different matter.'

A woman spoke – Rebecca's strong, resonant voice, hushed now and low. 'But Charles, supposing Decima—'

'Decima knows nothing, suspects nothing.'

'Then why did she invite that girl here?'

'A mere foil to divert attention from herself.'

'But supposing Decima should suspect—'

'My dear, Decima is totally absorbed in herself and always will be. Do you suppose she has any time for suspicions?'

'Charles . . .'

And then a silence broken only by a sharp intake of breath, a stifled exclamation and seconds later a small spent sigh.

Rachel took a step backwards in retreat. Her limbs were stiff and awkward as if suddenly released from a long paralysis, her thoughts spinning in shocked staccato patterns. Her first coherent reaction was that whatever happened they must not find her in the hall, must never guess that she had overheard Charles talking of a time when he might be 'free', speculating on Decima's suspicions, referring to her with such casual contempt.

She must hide. She had to think. Her mind was whirling

dizzily and all she was aware of was that Charles cared nothing for his wife's activities and would not risk losing Rebecca by making any move which might result in Daniel taking her away.

She opened the door of the drawing-room where she had talked to Rohan earlier and stumbled inside. Something moved on the hearth. As she jumped and stifled a cry of shock, a draught from the chimney made the dying fire throw out a shaft of light and she saw that the St Bernard had been stretched out on the hearthrug in slumber and that she had awoken him.

He gave a deep growl.

'It's all right, George,' she whispered. 'It's only me.'

He still growled, but now his tail was swaying from side to side. The firelight glinted in his eyes and made them look glazed and fierce.

She sank down in an armchair. Presently the dog relaxed too, still watching her, and they faced each other across the hearth. Beyond the dog stood the desk, its polished surface smooth, the red leather blotter glowing, the small calendar showing a date which was already three days old, the glass paperweight reflecting odd beams of the firelight.

Presently she stood up, moved restlessly over to the desk and altered the date on the calendar. It was now the morning of Saturday, the twelfth of September. Tonight at eight the dinner would begin to celebrate Decima's coming of age, and the next time the clocks struck midnight it would be to herald the beginning of Decima's twenty-first birthday. If anything were to happen to her, it would have to happen within the next twenty-four hours.

She replaced the calendar and then stopped to look at the desk. Surely something was missing. The top of the desk looked different in some way. She recalled her talk with Rohan in that same room a few hours ago, and as the scene came back into her mind she glanced at the smooth, empty surface of the table by the chair on the other side of the hearth.

Memory returned; the white ivory paper-knife with the razor-sharp edge was gone.

There was a void suddenly in the pit of her stomach; her

85

hands were clammy. Steady, she told herself. Don't jump to conclusions. Rohan probably moved it absentmindedly after I was gone.

She thought again of her conversation with him, the memory running through her mind like a strip of film. The knife had been on the desk by the paperweight and then Rohan had picked it up in his agitation, only to put it down again on the table a moment later. Then Rachel herself had picked it up and handled it for a short time. But she could clearly remember replacing it on the table by the chair.

She looked around, checking the mantelpiece, opening the drawers of the desk, even going over to the window-seat on the far side of the room. She was just pausing to examine the bric-à-brac in a small cabinet by the window when she suddenly knew beyond any doubt that she was no longer alone in the room.

She whirled round, her hand flying to her mouth as she saw the dark shadow watching her.

'Looking for something, Rachel?' inquired Daniel's cool voice from the doorway.

CHAPTER FIVE

I

He came into the room, his feet soundless on the soft carpet and closed the door behind him. The dog's tail thumped on the hearth in recognition, but Daniel ignored him.

'What are you doing down here at this hour?' His voice was still polite but the hard edge to it was unmistakable. Rachel was aware suddenly of the power of his presence, his ability to take command of a scene merely by entering a room.

'I couldn't sleep.' Her fingers were automatically drawing her dressing-gown closer around her. 'I came downstairs to look for a book I thought I'd left here.'

'I see,' he said and she knew he disbelieved her. 'And have you found it?'

'No. No, I—'

'What was it called?'

There was a small, deadly pause. She was completely unable to think of any title whatsoever.

'It was just a novel,' she stammered. 'I don't remember the title. It had a dark green cover with black lettering.'

'I'll help you look for it.'

'No, please . . . I'm not even sure that I left it in here.' Her self-possession was ebbing so fast that she almost felt she might turn and run from the room if he persisted in questioning her about the book. Emotional claustrophobia overwhelmed her; she began to move swiftly over to the door, but he was nearer the doorway than she was and in three strides he was there before her.

She stopped.

'What's the matter?' he said. 'You look very shaken. What's been happening?'

The impossibility of telling him that she had eavesdropped on Charles and Rebecca made her say the first thing that came into her head. 'What are *you* doing down here?' she demanded. 'Why were you still up?'

'I never go to bed before midnight,' he said shortly. 'I've been in the library reading and when I left to go upstairs just now I thought I heard sounds from this room.'

She found to her horror that she had nothing to say. She felt the colour suffuse her neck and creep upwards to her face, and it seemed as if all the self-consciousness of the past had combined in one enormous moment of embarrassment and diffidence. The brass handle of the door was cool against her palm. She tried to turn it but he put his hand over hers and stopped her.

'I want to talk to you.'

This was no scene played for Decima's benefit. Decima was upstairs behind her locked door. No matter how ambiguous his attitude might have seemed that afternoon in the wheelhouse, there could be no ambiguity this time in the drawing-room with the door closed to the world beyond and the fire dying in the grate.

'Perhaps it could wait till tomorrow,' she said, the old mixture of pride and fear and a dozen other muddled emotions making her withdraw from him although she longed for him to contradict her and force her to stay. 'I'm very tired.'

During past encounters with other men this had always been the point at which her involuntary coolness had resulted in her being left alone to regret her words. The man would have been either offended or disheartened; either he had never cared sufficiently to persist in overriding her request, or else he had never had the perspicacity to see that the apparent rejection was not a rejection at all but merely a craving for reassurance. Every man she had ever known well before had always chosen this moment to turn and walk away.

'Tired?' said Daniel. 'I thought you said you were so restless you had to come downstairs for a book? Come and sit down for a moment and tell me why you look as if you'd seen a ghost.'

'I – it was nothing.' But she allowed herself to turn from the door and sink down on the sofa beside the hearth. 'The house was so still that I became foolish and started imagining I heard noises and saw shapes in the shadows.'

He sat down on the sofa beside her; the springs creaked softly beneath his weight and then were still.

'Did Decima say anything?' he said at last.

'About the scene in the wheelhouse? No, nothing.'

'Nothing at all?'

'Nothing.'

So perhaps after all he was merely interested in Decima, curious to find out her reaction to the scene in the wheelhouse. Standing up blindly she moved back to the door. 'You'll excuse me, but I really mustn't stay . . . I'll find my book in the morning.'

But he was already standing up to follow her. Wanting only to escape from him now, she stepped quickly into the hall and was already past the threshold when she saw to her horror that Charles and Rebecca were just leaving the library.

She stopped.

Behind her Daniel too was motionless and she heard his sharp intake of breath. Across the hall Charles hesitated, his fingers still on the doorhandle as he drew it shut, and Rebecca, her cheeks hot, stared at Rachel.

There was a silence. Then:

'So you two are up late as well,' said Charles. 'Or did something bring you downstairs, Rachel?' He had noticed her shabby dressing-gown.

She suddenly realized that her face was still flushed from the encounter with Daniel. No doubt both Charles and Rebecca would think that she and Daniel had had some kind of rendez-vous in the drawing-room . . . She could feel the colour deepening in her cheeks and then Daniel was stepping past her towards his sister, his movements easy and relaxed.

'Rachel was looking for a book she'd left behind earlier this evening.' He was composed and untroubled. Once again he had entered a scene and blandly assumed control of the situation.

'Are you coming upstairs, now, Rebecca? Or shall I see you tomorrow morning?'

The words drew an innuendo which was a mere nuance as thin as a razor-edge but the tone of his voice gave the implication an uncomfortable depth.

'I don't know what that remark's supposed to mean,' said Charles much too quickly. 'What are you trying to imply, Daniel?'

'Why, merely that I'm going to bed myself and wondered if she intended to do likewise! What else could I mean?' He was mocking Charles, entangling him in verbal snares. 'Goodnight.'

'Wait!'

'Yes?'

Charles suddenly became aware of Rachel's presence and stopped. There was another awkward pause.

'If you'll excuse me . . .' Rachel muttered, and hurried past the group with her eyes on the ground. She could feel their eyes watching her as she ran upstairs and stumbled along the corridor to her room, and then as she reached the sanctuary she wrenched open the door and slammed it shut after her in her relief.

She sat down, still breathing unevenly, but presently when she had recovered her breath she opened her door again and went back into the passage. Decima must be told of the over-heard conversation between Charles and Rebecca. Moving cautiously back down the passage Rachel hesitated outside the door of Decima's room and then hearing the sound of voices she moved onto the gallery. There was no one in the hall but she could hear them raised in argument. They must have gone back to the study, or perhaps to the library, for although she could hear the voices she was still too far away to distinguish what was being said.

She hesitated and then, realizing that this was a good oppor-tunity to see Decima without danger of discovery, she went back to the locked door.

'Decima! Decima, are you awake?' She knocked swiftly on the panels. 'Decima, wake up!'

There was movement within, the flare of a match, the flicker-ing of light beneath the door.

'Rachel?' called Decima nervously.

'Yes – can you let me in?'

'Just a moment.'

More noises, the soft padding of slippers, the turning of the key in the lock, and then Decima was facing her across the threshold.

'What is it?' Her voice was almost hostile. 'What do you want?'

This was not the welcome Rachel had expected. 'Can I come in for a moment?' she said uneasily. 'It's difficult to talk out here.'

Decima opened the door without a word.

'Has something happened, Decima?'

'Nothing.' She turned aside and went back to the bed. 'I've just decided to open the door to no one either tonight or tomorrow evening before the party.'

'Not even to me?'

'Not even to you.'

'You mean you no longer trust me?' Rachel was both astonished and angry. 'Oh come, Decima! Just because Daniel—'

'Deny you're attracted to him, then!' Decima flared, whirling round to face her. 'Deny it! But you won't deny it, because it's true. And if it's true then I no longer trust you.'

'You're being absurd,' said Rachel coolly. 'For goodness' sake, Decima, pull yourself together! You're being both melodramatic and hysterical.'

'Who are you to talk of melodrama?' Decima exclaimed furiously. 'You with your adolescent infatuation, your schoolgirl's crush—'

Rachel turned aside abruptly. 'There's nothing more to be said.'

'I'm beginning to think Rohan's the only one I can trust,' Decima blazed, still trembling, her blue eyes narrow and hard. 'He at least hates Daniel.'

Rachel didn't listen. She was so angry that she went out and slammed the door violently behind her, and it was not until she was back in her room again that she realized she had mentioned not one word to Decima of the conversation she had overheard between Charles and Rebecca.

And as she thought of Charles and Rebecca she remembered the sounds of argument she had heard a few minutes ago, and it occurred to her to wonder what was happening in the library where Charles had gone with his guests.

II

Rachel awoke early again and lay listening for a long while to the still house. At last, unable to bear her immobility a moment longer, she got up and went over to draw the curtains. The morning was pale and cool, the sun visible but remote. Soon the clouds would creep in from the Atlantic and form a grey world of sky and sea, but at present the sunlight was strong enough to give a greenish tinge to the moors and a blue darkness to the swaying sea.

Rachel dressed and went downstairs. The housekeeper was busy in the scullery and, after taking some hot water, Rachel withdrew to one of the rooms near the kitchen to wash. There was a supply of running water on the ground floor of the house and two bathrooms near the kitchen, but hot water still had to be heated in the kitchens and transported gallon by gallon to the nearest bathroom. It occurred to Rachel as she staggered beneath the weight of two enormous jugs of steaming water that people who deprecated the modern comforts of the twentieth century should try living for a time in a house with no hot running water and no electricity. When she had finished dressing it was still early, too early for Decima to have stirred from her bed. Rachel wondered if anyone else was up. After hesitating for a while she went downstairs again to the kitchens. No one was about. The housekeeper had disappeared. Rachel found some porridge simmering on the range, helped herself to a bowlful and put the kettle on for tea, but even by the time she had finished her meal no one had come to interrupt her. She was just about to take the dirty dishes out to the scullery to wash them when there was the sound of footsteps in the hall and the next moment Charles walked into the room.

He stopped abruptly when he saw her. He looked tired, she thought. His mouth was drawn and there were lines of exhaustion about his eyes so that he looked closer to fifty than a man not yet forty years old.

'Oh, it's you,' he said. 'Is Mrs Willie about? I want to talk to her about the arrangements for the dinner-party tonight.'

'No, she seems to have disappeared.'

'Perhaps she went back to her croft to cook Willie his breakfast.' He went through into the scullery and looked at the saucepan of porridge without enthusiasm. Presently he came back into the kitchen and stared out of the window at the backyard beyond.

Rachel waited awkwardly, wanting to escape yet not knowing how to do so without appearing rude. She was just rising to her feet a moment later when Charles said suddenly: 'I'd like to talk to you. Would you have any objection if we walked out a little way over the moors?'

Rachel was astonished. 'Why, yes – yes, if you like, Charles,' she managed to say. 'Do you want to go now?'

'If you don't mind.'

'No, of course not. I'll just run upstairs and get my coat.'

There was still no one about, no sign of movement from upstairs. In her room once more she found her coat and slipped it over her shoulders. Then, still wondering what Charles could intend to say to her, she went downstairs to the kitchens to rejoin him.

He was still standing by the window, his hands in his pockets. As she came in he turned to face her. 'All right?'

She nodded.

'Good.' He led the way outside and the cool soft air of the Highland seas fanned her cheek as she stepped into the sunlight. She drew a deep breath, savouring the breeze's freshness, and then followed Charles across the yard and up the hillside to the north of the house, past a cow nibbling at the short grass and a sow with six piglets in the meadow beyond. There was a potato patch and a row of cabbages by the small croft where Willie the gamekeeper lived with his wife, and then Charles was leading the way out to the moors and up onto the cliff which rose above the sands.

'I wanted to get out of the house,' he said. 'Then there's no chance of anyone eavesdropping.'

Remembering how she herself had eavesdropped yesterday

93

evening, Rachel immediately felt herself blush scarlet, but fortunately he was ahead of her and did not notice. They walked on until the ground no longer tilted uphill but ran evenly along the top of the cliffs. To their left came the roar of the sea as the surf thundered on the beach and to the right loomed the nearest of the mountains, its bare slopes arid and rocky in the clear light.

There was a ragged stone circle ahead, the relic of some ancient tribe. Charles selected one of the stones that had fallen to the ground and sat down on it.

'Cigarette, Rachel?'

'No, thanks.'

She watched him light the cigarette and then toss the match away onto the damp ground. The flame smouldered, flared for a minute and then died in a thin curl of smoke.

After a long moment, he said: 'Why did Decima invite you here?'

Rachel searched desperately for a plausible explanation. 'I – I was an old friend . . . I suppose – as it was her twenty-first birthday she felt she would like to see me again—'

'I don't believe that,' said Charles. 'I don't mean to say that you're lying, but I think you've been misled. You're so utterly dissimilar from Decima that I can't visualize her wanting to resurrect a schoolgirl friendship.'

'But—'

'Decima hadn't contacted you since her marriage, had she? Why would she suddenly decide to do so?'

'I'm sorry, Charles, but I just don't understand what you're driving at. As far as I know—'

'But you know so little, don't you?' he said. 'You don't know anything at all.' His fingers were unsteady, she noticed with a shock; the hand which held the cigarette was shaking. There was a long pause. Then: 'I've been very foolish,' he said at last. 'I must have been quite mad. But it's not always easy to be as clever and wise as one always imagines oneself to be, is it? Sometimes you don't even realize how foolish you've been until it's too late to draw back.'

She could think of nothing to say. Below them the ocean

94

roared far away beneath the cliffs and the clouds were billowing towards them from the horizon.

'I've been having an affair with Rebecca,' he said suddenly. 'I know you're aware of that because Daniel told me last night that he had seen you outside the library listening to the conversation I was having with her.'

'I—' Guilt and horror made speech impossible. She could only stare at him with burning eyes while rage against Daniel throbbed through her mind.

'Daniel was angry,' said Charles as if this explained everything. 'We were all angry. We had an exhausting, abortive, endless quarrel which left us all drained of any vestige of emotion.' He drew on his cigarette. 'After it was all over, I felt as if I'd been shaken to my senses after six weeks of foolish illusions. And then I began to wonder what Decima had said to you and why you were here and I resolved to speak to you as soon as I could to tell you the truth and find out how far this situation had been misrepresented to you.'

His sincerity was almost painful. Rachel could hardly bear to look at him.

'I love Decima,' he said. 'I always have. I think it would be true to say that I loved her even more after we were married than before. Perhaps you find it hard to understand why I love her so much when we really have very little in common; we share no interests, come from different backgrounds, even different generations. But that makes no difference. After that terrible quarrel with the Careys last night I realized that in spite of all that had happened nothing had changed. I would never consent to losing her. How could I? Our marriage at the moment is a mockery, but I would rather have her on those terms than not have her at all.' He was staring down at his cigarette, his shoulders hunched, his limbs tensed and motionless. 'Besides,' he said after a moment, 'the situation as it exists now between us could hardly get any worse. After thinking about it all night, I came to the conclusion that if I made a great effort and did all I could, things might still work out. If I could take Decima abroad for a while – if we could get away from this place, this prison, this enforced confinement far from any normal civilized way of life, then I think there might be some hope for us. Shut away up here one tends to forget what a normal life under normal conditions is like. If we could go abroad for a while and come to know one another again, then perhaps there could be children. We could settle in the country near Oxford, perhaps. There are some beautiful houses north of Banbury.'

'Decima will never leave Ruthven,' Rachel heard herself say.

'No, she doesn't want to leave – she doesn't want to face the normal world, can't you see? She had such an appalling child-hood and adolescence trailing round the world in the wake of her promiscuous mother that she wants nothing but to retreat from anything that remotely resembles that way of life. But if only she could be shown that life in the outside world is nothing to be feared, then I think she would be happy to settle some-where away from Ruthven. At the moment she is rejecting all the values of a normal world and burying herself in this tomb – she's destroying herself, destroying me, destroying everything I've ever wanted.'

'But Charles, you talk as if Decima was mentally unhinged! Surely—'

'Not mentally unhinged, but there's something definitely wrong in her psychological make-up, can't you understand?' His eyes were wide and dark, his face strained. 'What girl of twenty-one, who could have the world at her feet, would choose to seclude herself in a place like this? Why should any normal girl refuse to live with her husband barely six months after they were married? I wanted her to consult a doctor, but she refused and seemed to withdraw from me still further until it seemed she was building up a store of mythical grievance against me in her mind. And yet I loved her! I tried and tried to reason with her, but there was nothing I could do. I gave her everything she wanted, spent much more money than I should have done, and still all she did was complain about our brief term-time life at Oxford and criticize my Oxonian friends. She seemed to take pleasure in embarrassing me, in making me as unhappy as possible. Last winter I let her go home to Ruthven early to pre-pare for Christmas before I arrived, but I missed her so much while she was away that I couldn't bear to be separated from her again. I can't begin to describe to you the misery and frustration and hopelessness of it all. I didn't know it was possible to be so unhappy.

'But we went on from day to day, still together. Some days were better than others. And then, this summer, when Daniel wrote to say he and Rebecca were in Scotland, I asked them to Ruthven in the hope that a glimpse of the outside world which they might present would in some way help Decima. And so the Careys came to Ruthven.

'I suppose it wasn't surprising that I should be attracted to Rebecca. She was everything that Decima was not, intellectual, passionate and intense. She was interested in my work, enjoyed my company and – it was obvious – admired me. You can imagine the effect this would have on me after the life I had been living with Decima. No doubt I shouldn't offer excuses for myself, but Rebecca gave me all that I had lacked for the past two years. I lost all hold on my restraint, my common sense, my self-control. I lost sight of everything. I never even noticed that Daniel found Decima attractive or that she had decided to play around with him. I was well accustomed to ignore all her empty gestures of flirtation at Oxford, and well used to the fact that most men found my wife attractive. Even if I had noticed I might not have taken it seriously, and as it was I was too absorbed with Rebecca to notice anyone else.

'So Decima became involved with Daniel – and found she had taken on more than she bargained for. Daniel wasn't one of the fresh-faced students she'd been so accustomed to dazzling at Oxford! And Daniel was the last man to allow her to call the tune and set the pace of their relationship. Daniel knew what he wanted and if Decima wasn't interested in playing the game by his rules, then he certainly wasn't going to bend over backward to do as *she* wished!'

'So Daniel never had an affair with Decima.' She was dizzy suddenly, faint with the vastness of relief. 'He never had an affair with her.'

Charles raised his eyebrows. 'No, you misunderstand – I see I explained myself badly. Decima wanted a flirtation with

Daniel for her own satisfaction and amusement – in other words, an attachment which would never get as far as the bedroom. But Daniel wasn't interested in getting involved merely to gratify Decima's ego. So he took control of the situation and dictated his own terms and Decima, caught off balance, no doubt, and taken by surprise, allowed herself to be dictated to.'

'But you said Decima was cold – cold and withdrawn! I don't believe she would ever have had an affair with Daniel! I just don't believe it!'

'My dear, he told me last night that they were lovers. He told me himself.'

The roar of the surf suddenly seemed much too close. The oppressiveness of that welling of sound made the sea blur before her eyes and she turned away instinctively to stare inland over the barren moors and the harsh lines of the mountains.

'Last night after you'd left us in the hall we went back into the study. Daniel had made it clear that he knew all about Rebecca's affair with me, but I had been so blind as to imagine he had no idea what was going on. I was angry with him for implying as much in your presence and once we were in the library I told him so. It was then that Daniel said you knew anyway as he had seen you listening at the door – he said it was perfectly obvious to anyone what was going on. That, of course, made me even angrier and we started to quarrel. Rebecca tried to speak up for me from time to time, but he wouldn't let her and she would rather argue with God than argue with Daniel. So Daniel began to speak as if he were the prosecuting counsel at a trial and I the prisoner at the bar.

'To begin with I was so furious that I could hardly listen to a word he said. Then gradually I began to realize that much of what he said was true, and I began to feel sick and ill. He told me that I was to blame for the situation at Ruthven, that it was my fault that Decima had behaved the way she had, that I had behaved like a middle-aged fool over his sister. "You moan to my sister of how your wife misunderstands you," he said, "but how much effort have you made to correct the situation? Aren't you just too content to sit back and let Decima go her own way while you go yours? You weep that you loved your wife and got nothing in return, but how far did you go to offer anything apart from the honour of bearing your name and the dubious pleasures of your narrow academic social circles? Did you protest at Decima's flirtations at Oxford? Oh no, you were too busy sitting back and getting a vicarious sense of enjoyment by watching her play with her admirers and eventually send them packing! You were so smug and self-satisfied with your beautiful wife, so damned sure she was too cold ever to be actually unfaithful to you! You basked in the reflected glory of other men's admiration for her! You were too vain to care that she was driven to amuse herself with others because you couldn't keep her fully amused yourself!"

'I couldn't contain myself any longer. I shouted at him: "Who are you to preach to me, Daniel Carey? You come here at my express invitation and yet think nothing of abusing my hospitality in the most shameful way imaginable! Do you think I hadn't noticed that Decima has been flirting with you?" To be honest, I hadn't noticed this until Rohan pointed it out to me yesterday morning, but even then I assumed it was a mere casual flirtation and I was far too involved with Rebecca to ask Daniel to leave. "Just deny that you haven't tried to persuade Decima to have an affair with you!" I shouted at him. "Just try to deny it!"

'And he said coolly, with such scorn as I could never put into words, "Of course I don't deny it. Why should I? I decided to teach you both a lesson, Charles! I thought it was high time someone showed Decima what it was like to be used as a pawn, a means of amusement – I thought it was high time she had a dose of her own medicine! And I thought it was high time someone knocked down the walls of egoism and vanity you've built around yourself, time someone showed you that your wife wasn't as cold as you liked to think she was!"

'I couldn't quite grasp what he was saying at first. I said: "What do you mean?"

'And he said, "You don't think I'd let any woman use *me* as a plaything, do you? I dictate my own terms, and Decima hardly paused to question them. She became my mistress some time ago.'

'I stared at him. I couldn't even think coherently. And suddenly all I knew was that this man had taken my wife and I had stood by and let it happen because of a temporary infatuation with another woman. I felt ill and dizzy, as if someone had taken an axe and smashed my world to smithereens. After a while I managed to say to them both, "You will leave this house on Sunday morning and I never want to see either of you again." And I left them together in the library and somehow managed to find my way upstairs to my room.

'I tried to sleep, but all the time I kept thinking of what Daniel had said and every time I went over his words again, the more truth I seemed to see in them. I resolved that once the Careys were gone I would take Decima away and try to start all over again. I realized that I loved her and wanted her still, and in the light of this realization my attraction to Rebecca seemed very shallow and meaningless.'

He stopped. The world was still. The clouds had blotted out the sun now and were wreathing the mountaintops with soft, ghostly fingers.

'But what was Rebecca's reaction when you told them both to leave?' Rachel heard herself ask. 'Wasn't she very upset?'

'I didn't stay to see her reaction. All I knew was that I never wanted to see either of them again.' He buried his head in his hands for a moment. 'Rohan was right,' he said after a while. 'He distrusted them from the first. There are some people like that, I suppose. They're destructive, dangerous people leaving a trail of disaster behind them. Once they're out of our lives, perhaps we'll at last be able to return to normal.'

It was raining, the light sea-mist fresh against Rachel's skin. The damp moistness was somehow soothing, and she faced towards the sea to meet it.

Charles stood up. 'We'd better go back.'

They left the stone circle and started back along the cliffs. For a time neither of them spoke.

'I'm sorry to have burdened you with all this,' Charles said at last, 'but I didn't know what you were thinking or what conclusions you had drawn from the knowledge that you had, and I felt it important that you should know the truth.'

'Yes,' said Rachel. 'Yes, I quite understand. Thank you.'

'I seem to be totally unable to communicate with Decima at the moment. She refuses to talk to me. I was wondering if she'd said anything to you.'

'No, she was very reluctant to talk to me last night. I only noticed that she seemed very upset over Daniel.'

'Well yes,' said Charles. 'I've no doubt she is . . . I'm hoping to God everything will be better after the Careys have gone. I wish now we could put off this damned dinnner-party tonight, but we've invited too many people from outside and it's too late now to get in touch with them.'

'Couldn't you phone them and cancel it?'

'Ruthven's not on the phone.'

'Oh no, how stupid of me. I forgot.'

They walked on for a few yards. Then:

'You asked me in the beginning why Decima invited me to Ruthven,' Rachel said. 'Why do *you* think she invited me, Charles?'

'I think possibly she may have fancied the notion of leaving me and marrying Daniel. She would have assumed I'd be most reluctant to divorce her and so she wanted a witness that I was committing adultery with Rebecca. Rohan, being my cousin, would naturally be averse to being a witness against me, so she found herself in need of inviting an outsider to Ruthven.'

'But did she know about you and Rebecca? I always had the impression she had no idea of this.'

'No, she knew all the time. Daniel said last night that she had known almost from the beginning – and found my infatuation amusing,' he added bitterly. 'Yes, she knew all right. I suppose I was so wrapped up in my feelings for Rebecca that it must have been patently obvious to everyone, even to Decima, who's usually too absorbed in her own affairs to notice the affairs of others.'

In Decima's eyes, Rachel thought, this would give Charles yet another motive for wanting to kill her, for he would then inherit her money and marry Rebecca. It was only surprising that she had never once mentioned it to Rachel. Perhaps she had been held back by some obscure pride; the fact that her husband was being unfaithful to her must have been a blow to her ego, no matter how amused she might have pretended to be to Daniel about the situation.

Yet it was almost impossible now for Rachel to imagine Charles planning to kill Decima. Perhaps it had all been some terrible figment of Decima's imagination. Perhaps Decima really was mentally disturbed.

They'll turn you against me, Decima had said. They'll try to prise you away from me, because you're the one person I can trust . . .

'I don't know what to think,' Rachel said aloud in despair. 'I simply don't know what to do.'

Charles swung round startled. Was it her imagination or did she really see a flash of suspicion in his eyes? Perhaps the whole scene had been played for calculated effect, to deceive her. Perhaps it was all a masquerade.

'It's nothing,' she said. 'I suddenly felt so confused.'

'I understand – I'm sorry. I almost forgot you would be fond of Decima. It must be very upsetting for you to hear bad reports of her.'

Rachel said nothing.

They were in sight of the house now, following the path down the hillside past the croft, the pigsty and the cow. The housekeeper was in the yard taking in some washing. As they approached she caught sight of them and withdrew to the shelter of the back porch to wait till they were nearer.

'Mrs Willie looks worried,' said Charles. 'I hope nothing's wrong.'

They reached the yard and crossed it to the porch. The housekeeper started to speak almost as soon as they were within earshot. 'I was never so glad to see you, Professor,' she was saying, and anxiety made her soft Highland accent broader so that it sounded Irish. 'What should I be doing about preparing the dinner for tonight? Mrs Mannering's just taken the boat and gone off to sea without telling me what arrangements she wanted me to make, and—'

'Gone off to sea?' cried Charles in amazement. 'When was this, for God's sake?'

'Maybe ten minutes ago, sir. I heard the engine of the boat and saw her at the wheel heading away from the shore.'

'Was she alone?'

'No, sir. She went with your cousin, Mr Quist.'

III

Charles was quick to pull himself together. Moving forward into the kitchens with the housekeeper, he surveyed the food in the pantry and then embarked on a discussion of how the venison should be cooked. After a moment's hesitation Rachel went outside again and walked round to the front of the house, but the motorboat was nowhere to be seen and the vast expanse of the ocean stretched uninterrupted to the horizon. She stood still, undecided what she should do, and as she paused she wondered in astonishment where Decima and Rohan had gone and why they had chosen to walk out of the house on the very morning of the party, when their help would be needed in making the necessary preparations. If she were Charles, Rachel thought, she would be very angry indeed.

Someone was calling her name. Turning abruptly she saw Charles coming towards her from the back of the house and she retraced her steps to meet him.

'There's no sign of them, is there?' he demanded, and when she shook her head he said tightly: 'I don't know what the hell they think they're doing but I can only assume they've just gone for a short spin and will be back before long. I think the best we can do is merely to carry on with the preparations and do as much as we can.'

'Yes – yes, of course . . . What would you like me to do?'

'Well, I hate to ask one of my own guests to do anything at all, but I wonder if you could possibly pick some flowers and arrange them in the hall? We'll be dining in the hall tonight, of course. I must find Daniel and ask him to help me set up the long banquet table . . . Do you think you can manage the flowers?'

'Yes, don't worry, Charles. And if there's anything else I can do, just let me know.'

After he had gone, she walked down into the overgrown garden and examined the selection of flowers, but it was late in the year and summer had already left the Highlands so that there were few flowers to choose from. There were some hardy blue-petalled shrubs beneath the shelter of the stone wall at one end of the garden but the stems were tough beneath her fingers and in the end she decided to go back into the house for a pair of scissors. It was already beginning to rain again; the sky was heavy with billowing clouds blowing in from the sea and the few streaks of blue which remained were pale and cold and far away.

Charles and the housekeeper were still in the pantry; Rachel found a pair of heavy shears in one of the drawers of the kitchen table and wandered back into the hall. She felt curiously abstracted from reality, as if she were moving in a dream and was powerless to control her own fate. It was as if forces around her were manipulating her at will, pulling her this way and that and finally tossing her adrift on the strong current of a swift-flowing river which was rushing her headlong towards some destination as terrible as it was unknown. She could feel her own helplessness as clearly as she could feel that dreadful propulsion towards the hidden future which lay waiting for them all. She paused again in the huge hall and listened to the silence, and even as she realized at last how frightened she was, she heard the sound of weeping coming from the drawing-room close at hand.

The door was ajar. With her fingers pressing against the panels she opened it still wider and glanced into the room.

'Danny?' said Rebecca sharply as she saw the door open and then, as she realized it was Rachel, she turned aside without a word and buried her face in her arms again.

Rachel did not know whether to move forward or to retreat. In the end she remained where she was, one hand still on the door handle, and said hesitantly: 'If there's anything I can do – shall I find Daniel for you?'

Rebecca lifted her head so fiercely that Rachel had a stab of shock. Her eyes, brilliant with tears, were suddenly blazing with anger, and her limbs were trembling. 'You!' she cried.

'You! You've caused enough trouble! You leave Daniel alone! Why did you come to this place anyway, except to spy and cause trouble? That's why Decima asked you to come, wasn't it? To spy on me and Charles so that she could drag Charles' name through the mud in a divorce petition? And now you've turned Charles against me and towards Decima again because you want to keep Decima from Daniel – because you want Daniel for yourself! Why, you silly, stupid fool! Do you think Daniel cares a damn for either of you? Do you think he cares for Decima's shallowness, her coldness, her boring trivial feminine mind? And do you think he cares any more for you with your dreary old clothes and your spinsterish mannerisms, your gaucheness and pseudo-intellectualism? And now because of you and what you've done, Charles has told us to leave and my whole world is over and finished—'

Rachel at last found her tongue. The rage was so vast within her that it impaired her speech and her voice was low and harsh and uneven. 'You're being melodramatic, over-emotional and utterly absurd, only you're so in love with your role as rejected heroine that you can't bear to look at the situation as it really is!' Her hands were clenched so tightly that they hurt; her nails dug into her palms. 'I've never spied on you and Charles! I don't care how much of a fool you care to make of yourself over a married man in the name of free love or whatever quasi-intellectual line of philosophy you happen to believe in – why should I care? It's nothing to do with me! And if you think Decima asked me up here to spy on you two, you must be mad! Decima was far too engrossed in Daniel to care what you did with her husband when her back was turned – she merely invited me here to keep Rohan out of her way. And if you think I would ever be interested in a man who sleeps with his host's wife – or any other woman who happens to be available – you couldn't be more wrong! You can keep your precious brother! Let him take you as far away from Ruthven as it's possible to go, for I don't care if I never see either of you again!'

Rebecca was on her feet, her face white, her movements unsteady, her eyes wide and dark and hard. 'That's what Charles said.' Her voice was little more than a whisper. And then suddenly she was screaming, her face distorted, her eyes narrow slits of rage: 'I hate you all, do you hear? I hate every one of you! I hate Decima and I hate you and I hate that fool Quist and I hate Charles – Charles more than any of you! Charles Mannering, the noble, distinguished, celebrated professor, the lying, weak, cowardly bastard who tells me that he's so sorry – yes, *so sorry*, but he's made a mistake and he doesn't want to divorce Decima after all and marry me – he's *so sorry*, but actually he doesn't want to see me again because I've served my purpose, just as if I were some tart or some harebrained little student who had a crush on him at Oxford! "I'm so sorry," he says! My God, I'll make him sorry! I'll teach him what it is to be sorry. I'll—'

She stopped.

Behind Rachel the door was softly closed.

'You'd better go to your room, Rebecca,' said Daniel without emotional inflection. 'You forget that we're not leaving till tomorrow.'

There was a long silence. Rebecca was staring at him, and Rachel suddenly found she had to sit down. Daniel was motionless. Presently he held out his hand to his sister.

'I'll take you upstairs.'

'It's all right.' She was crying again, pushing past Rachel and stumbling towards Daniel.

He opened the door for her. 'I'll come upstairs presently.'

She made no reply. They could hear the harshness of her sobs as she moved across the hall to the stairs, and then Daniel closed the door and there was silence.

After a while he said: 'It seems I was mistaken.'

She stared at him, not understanding and outside the squall broke and the rain hurled itself against the windowpane in an ecstasy of violence.

'I misjudged the kind of person you were.' He crossed to the fireplace and was still again, looking at her. 'You told Charles about Decima and myself, didn't you?'

She was wild-eyed, mesmerized by his stillness, appalled by his controlled anger. 'No,' she heard herself say, 'Rohan told Charles. I had nothing to do with it. It was Rohan.'

'Rohan or you – it's the same thing, isn't it? For a long time I was puzzled about why you had been asked to Ruthven and then at last I realized that Quist had manoeuvred it. He thought you could be useful to him – and of course you were.'

'Useful?' She felt dizzy, confused. 'I don't understand.'

'Don't tell me you hadn't realized that Quist is infatuated with Decima and would do anything to drive a wedge between her and any man she happened to be interested in?'

'I—'

'He hated me from the first but was powerless to do anything about the situation. To make matters worse, Charles was so absorbed in Rebecca that he didn't care what his wife was doing with me! So Quist conceived the idea of inviting an outsider here whom he could use and manipulate to play the four of us off against each other with the result that Decima and Charles would be reconciled and Rebecca and I would be sent away. Which is exactly what has happened.'

'But what you say isn't true!' said Rachel loudly, struggling with the tangled web in which she found herself. 'It was Decima who invited me here – Rohan had nothing to do with it! Nothing! It was Decima, Decima, Decima! Can't you understand! And Rohan isn't infatuated with her anyway – you're the one who's so infatuated with her that you're driven to imagine these preposterous schemes and ideas!'

'So you *are* jealous,' he said, 'I thought you were. You told Charles that Decima had been having an affair with me and Quist backed you up to the hilt. And Charles is so weak and so easily swayed that the two of you managed to convince him that he'd have no peace of mind till Rebecca and I left this house.'

'It's not true – not true—'

'You hate Decima's guts, don't you? You'd see her dead if you could!'

'No, no – I'm not like that—'

'Well, you've been wasting your energy being jealous! Decima's not my mistress and never has been. I told Charles last night that she was but it was a lie because I wanted to shake him . . . He's so damned smug, so damned self-righteous, so bloody satisfied in the belief that his wife would never be un-faithful to him! I saw that he had made up his mind to be rid of us so I didn't care what I said or how much I hurt him so long as I dragged him down from the pompous little pedestal he had built for himself. I was tired of the way he was using my sister, tired of his affectations and complacency!'

'You hate him because he's Decima's husband!'

'Decima! I care nothing for Decima! All I ask is to be rid of her – she's a danger to me, a menace to my future plans. If she gets Charles to use his influence in revenge—'

'I don't believe you,' Rachel heard herself say, and her voice was no longer steady. 'You had an affair with Decima, and now you suspect her of preferring Rohan – or even Charles. You're so unaccustomed to a woman losing interest in you before you lose interest in her that you have to resort to wild flights of imagination—'

'You don't know what you're talking about.'

'I just don't believe you never had an affair with Decima!'

'I don't care what you believe! Why should I? What are you to me? I thought at first you were different, but now I see you're the same as a thousand other women, petty, jealous and mun-dane. The hell with you! Go on back to your so-called platonic friend Rohan Quist and vent your stupid small-minded jealousy on his obsession with Decima Mannering, for God knows I've no further use for you.'

And he was gone as quietly as he had come, leaving nothing behind him but the squalling of the rain on the windows and the howl of the sea wind far away.

IV

She went to her room and stayed there. She shut the door and pushed a chair against it to hold it fast in lieu of a key, and she drew the curtains to shut out the tortured convulsions of the weather and the appalling bleakness of the barren landscape. And then she lay down on her bed in the cool twilight and cried till her throat ached and her eyes were too swollen to see. Her face became hot and flushed with her tears, but after a while she became aware of how cold she was and how much she longed for the heat of a fire.

She got up, stooped to examine the grate, but there was nothing there but ashes and the scuttle by the hearth had only a few small pieces of wood in it. Shivering, she drew back the curtains and stared dry-eyed at the scene before her. It had stopped raining. The squall had died, but there was a mist clinging to the mountains and she could hear the hum of the strong wind as it swept in from the sea.

She shivered again. Perhaps there would be more fuel in Decima's room, and some matches too to set the fire alight. She started to wonder if Decima and Rohan had come back from their trip to sea, but that only made her think of Daniel again and her eyes filled with tears. She tried to dash them away, but they only fell the faster and she was still crying as she pulled aside the barricade, opened her door and stepped out into the corridor.

It was very quiet. Stifling her sobs, she went down the corridor to Decima's room at the far end and fumbled with the latch.

There were glowing embers in the grate; evidently Decima had lit the fire that morning, and the room was still warm and comfortable. Rachel closed the door behind her and locked it before sinking down on the hearthrug to build the fire to a warmer blaze, and within minutes the flames were leaping up the chimney and the cold was slowly ebbing from her limbs.

She sat there for a long while. There was a curious burning in her mind, as if some rich and valuable vein of thought had been hacked off and obliterated by some frenzied act of destruction. Her other thoughts were dim and unresponsive, her other emotions dulled by pain and anaesthetized by shock. All she was conscious of was this great searing sense of loss for which there was no cure, no solution. 'I never loved him,' she said to herself again and again. 'It was an infatuation. He was right and I was jealous and foolish and stupid. He despises me.'

But she had loved him. She had timidly reached out towards him, her longing overcoming all her shyness and reserve and fear, and her love had been wrenched from her, twisted by cruel hands and flung back, a crippled, shameful, distorted thing, into her face. She felt too crushed, too humiliated and too full of pain even to acknowledge that the love she had felt had been as deep as any of which she was capable. She could only acknowledge the twisted distortion which had been flung back at her, and could only tell herself numbly that she had been deluded and absurd.

'It was an infatuation,' she said aloud to the hard tongues of flame in the grate. 'I was foolish. I never loved him.'

And the pain of loss was a raw gaping wound from which it seemed the throbbing would never die, and the grief was a great barren waste which stretched as far as the eye could see.

'I wasn't in love,' she said. 'I was infatuated. I was mistaken. It was all a mistake.'

And it seemed to her even as she listened to the words that the house around her and landscape beyond the window perfectly represented the desolation of her mind, the negation of all warmth and light and the presence only of arid starkness and a waste of isolation.

She got up and went to the window, as if by gazing out on that bleak landscape she could somehow gaze into her own mind, and as she moved she brushed the cushion from the window-seat to the floor. She stooped automatically to pick it up and then she noticed that on the window-seat there was a slim leather-bound volume which the cushion had concealed.

It was a diary.

She picked it up, but her fingers were still unsteady and it slithered through them to the floor and fell open at her feet. She stooped, and as she picked up the book she saw that the writing was not Decima's at all but a stormy tempestuous scrawl forming emotional uneven sentences.

Her eyes read isolated words even before her mind could stop them. 'Charles said . . . I told Charles I felt . . . Charles and I made love . . . Charles promised . . . Charles . . .'

There were intimate descriptions, passages of avowed love, ecstatic words of praise.

Rachel shut the book tightly and put it back beneath the

cushion. It was only when she turned away once more towards the fire that it occurred to her numbed brain to wonder why Rebecca Carey's diary should be so carefully concealed in Decima's room.

CHAPTER SIX

I

Rohan and Decima didn't come back. The long morning drifted
into a cold grey afternoon and still there was no sign of them.
At some time after three Rachel slipped into an exhausted sleep
on the hearthrug in Decima's room but no one interrupted her
and no one came to see where she was.

When she awoke it was dark and the fire was dying in the
grate. For one long moment she lay still, too stiff and cramped
to move, and then memory flooded back into her mind with a
stab of pain and she sat up, ignoring the ache in her limbs and
the dry burning of her eyes. Tonight was the night of the dinner
party, the night when sixteen guests at eight-thirty would be
arriving at Ruthven to dine in the great hall below. Tonight
was the eve of Decima's twenty-first birthday, the last night of
the Careys' stay at Ruthven, the last time that Rachel would see
Daniel. Tonight was the night of masquerade, of playing a part,
of letting no one know that her mind was still in the grip of that
great aching sense of loss that cast out all other thought and
emotion.

No one must ever know, was all she could tell herself. No one
must ever find out.

She stood up painfully, and moved to the door. It was so dark
in the corridor that she had to pause for a moment to get her
bearings, and then she set off in the direction of her room with
one hand against the wall so that she would know when she
reached the door. A minute later she was sitting on her own
bed and struggling to light the lamp.

Mrs Willie had obviously been much too busy cooking to go
around lighting fires in the bedrooms; the ashes were still grey
in the grate and the room seemed bitterly cold and damp.
Rachel drew on her overcoat and looked at herself in the mirror.

She saw a stranger with dishevelled hair and bloodshot eyes

swollen with weeping. Her skin seemed blotched, her expression empty of all feeling. She stared at herself for a long time and then, lamp in hand, went back to Decima's room for a box of matches and a log for the fire.

It was six o'clock when she managed to get the fire alight. She desperately wanted hot water to bathe her face but she was afraid of meeting the housekeeper in the kitchen, afraid of anyone seeing her before she had had a chance to mend her appearance a little. Presently she used some of the cold water in the ewer to wash her face, and then she spent some time combing and rearranging her hair before venturing downstairs to fetch hot water.

The hall looked beautiful, the long banquet table aglow with white linen and silver cutlery and red candles waiting to be lit. Someone had completed the task which Charles had allotted to her, for there were flowers in tall vases on the chest and tables at the side of the hall and a small arrangement on the banquet table among the two epergnes. Four lamps were burning and huge fires were blazing in the enormous twin fireplaces on either side of the hall.

Charles came out of the library just as she stepped into the hall and paused to look at the scene. There was no escaping him.

'Hullo,' he said. 'Where have you been? I tried to find you a while ago and had no success.'

'I'm so sorry, Charles – I – I didn't feel too well . . . Please forgive me for not doing the flowers—'

'No, that doesn't matter. I picked them later and Mrs Willie arranged them when she had a spare minute. I say, are you all right? You look very pale.'

'Yes, I'm much better now, thank you. I was just going to get some hot water to wash with before I change. Are Decima and Rohan back yet?'

'No, they're not. I don't know where the hell they've got to. I can only suppose that the storm caught them at sea and forced them to head for Kyle of Lochalsh for shelter. The storm's stopped here but it may still be strong over at Kyle and forcing them to stay in harbour there. I hope to God they get back before the guests start to arrive. It was a damnfool thing to do today of all days anyway – Decima at least, if not Rohan, ought to have been here to help with all the preparations . . . Rachel, are you sure you're all right? You certainly don't look well.'

'Yes, really, Charles, I'm quite all right now . . .' She made her escape, obtained her supply of hot water and set off back to her bedroom again before she should meet anyone else. There was a glow of light beneath Daniel's door as she passed it, but Rebecca's room was in darkness.

Perhaps Rebecca intended to spend the evening on her own.

It was only when Rachel reached her room again that she became aware of panic. How could she possibly face all those people whom she did not know and act as if nothing had happened? How could she be sociable and friendly and hospitable just as if nothing were wrong? And how could she even begin to think of facing Daniel again after all that had been said between them that morning?

Because no one must ever know, she thought. No one is ever going to know unless I'm weak and give myself away. And I'm not going to be weak and give in and hide myself in my room because I haven't enough courage to face the world at this particular time.

No one must ever know.

The evening loomed before her, an enormous obstacle which had to be surmounted before the tranquillity and relief of the day ahead. All she had to do was to get through this evening somehow. Once the evening was over she would be able to relax and recover herself.

She didn't know then how wrong she was. Afterwards, looking back, she decided that this was just as well, for if she had known then what was going to happen that evening she would never have left her room.

II

'But where are they?' cried Charles in exasperation. 'Why aren't they here? What's happened to them?'

The clock chimed half past seven. Rachel, seated tensely before the hearth of one of the big fires in the hall, made no reply, and presently Charles in an agony of suspense paced to the front door and opened it to stare out to sea.

'There's a boat coming in now . . .' He stepped outside, shutting the door behind him, and Rachel was left alone before the hearth in the silent hall.

A door closed somewhere far away upstairs; there were voices, a murmur of conversation, the sound of footsteps on the stairs.

Rachel did not turn around. At last when they were behind her she glanced up and tried to force out a stiff 'good evening' but Daniel moved past her without a glance in her direction and Rebecca went over to the table on a pretence of examining the silverware.

Rachel stared back into the flames.

'Someone's arriving,' said Daniel to his sister. 'There's a boat down by the quay.'

'Rohan and Decima?'

'I don't know. There's another boat out at sea heading in this direction. The guests are starting to arrive.'

'Supposing Decima doesn't come back?'

'Then Charles will look like a bloody fool, won't he?' said Daniel and opened the front door to stand outside on the porch.

The St Bernard, which had been closeted in the kitchen out of the way until he had escaped through the back door, lumbered solemnly into the room and settled himself comfortably at Rachel's feet before the fire. Mrs Willie, scurrying into the hall at the same moment with two large ashtrays, caught sight of him and gave an exclamation of annoyance.

'George, what are you doing in the hall? Come here at once, you bad dog!' And she stooped to smack his head and lay a firm hand on his collar.

The St Bernard growled.

'Let him be,' called Daniel from the door. 'He's no trouble. I'll see he's not a nuisance.'

'Just as you like, Mr Carey,' said the housekeeper with a shrug and disappeared again in the direction of the kitchen while the dog returned to his slumbers on the hearthrug.

'It's neither Decima nor Rohan,' said Rebecca who had been

watching from the window. 'It must be the first contingent of guests.'

And the next moment Charles had entered the room with the MacDonalds and Camerons from Kyle of Lochalsh and the party had begun.

Afterwards, Rachel's memories of that last dinner at Ruthven were blurred and she could remember only isolated scenes which seemed to have little or no connexion with each other. She could remember Charles saying – how many times? Three? Four? – that Decima had gone into Kyle of Lochalsh to do some last-minute shopping and had apparently been delayed there with Rohan. She could remember Robert Cameron saying that he had noticed the Ruthven boat moored in the harbour at Kyle, and the look of relief on Charles' face changing to one of anger as he began to wonder why Decima was deliberately delaying her return.

The Kincaids arrived from Skye soon after eight and finally Decima's lawyer, old Conor Douglas, from Cluny Gualach with his daughter, but still there was no sign of Decima and Rohan. Half past eight struck. Then a quarter to nine.

'We'd better dine, I think,' said Charles abruptly. 'There's no use in spoiling the dinner, and I've no doubt you're all hungry after your journey.'

Rachel could remember the glow of candles in silver candlesticks and the sparkle of champagne in the elegant glasses, but not the taste of the food, nor the order of the menu. She was sitting between one of the MacDonalds, a young man of about twenty-seven, and old Mr Douglas the lawyer, and all the time she was conscious of Decima's empty chair at one end of the long table and Rohan's vacant place directly opposite her. Daniel was far away, hidden from her almost entirely by one of the epergnes and a candelabrum of red candles, but sometimes during a lull in the conversation she could hear his voice travelling towards her from the other end of the table.

The dinner was finished at last, the speeches left unsaid. The guests lingered at the table over coffee and liqueurs, and the conversation rippled on inconsequentially, the guests mellow with good food and drink and almost forgetting that the guest of honour had never appeared to receive them. To Rachel, longing for the solitude of her room and an escape from the torture of making sociable conversation, it seemed as if the party would never end.

It was some time after ten when Decima and Rohan came back. They were laughing together up the garden path from the jetty, and it was not until Rohan flung wide the front door and strode into the room that Rachel realized they were both dead drunk.

III

'Good evening, everyone,' said Decima, mocking them all. 'How kind of you to come. Please excuse me not being here to greet you but Rohan wanted to make love to me and I had to explain that I can't be unfaithful to my husband, even though he's been sleeping with Rebecca Carey for the last few weeks, because he wants a reconciliation with me and he's promised to send the Careys away tomorrow. Why, Charles darling, how beautiful the hall looks! So sorry I wasn't here to help ... Rachel, you look awful! What's the matter? Hasn't Daniel bothered to give you his best smile today? Daniel, you really should be more considerate!'

'Charles,' said Daniel to his host, 'your wife's as drunk as a barmaid. You'd better take her upstairs.'

'Why, listen, Charles!' jeered Rohan. 'Listen to who's giving you advice! It's the guest who tried to seduce your wife under your own roof, Charles! Why don't you ask him to put Decima to bed for you? I'll tell you why you don't ask him, Charles. It's because you're so god-damned proud, Charles, that you can't admit you could ever be in the position of the fooled husband! You think you're God, don't you, Charles, God's gift to culture, to academic life, to women, to the whole world, but hell to all that, Charles, you're not God's gift to your wife!'

Charles was white to the lips, shocked speechless.

Daniel was on his feet, his hands gripping Rohan's arm as he tried to lead him away. Around the table the guests were frozen with shock, as silent and motionless as if they had been carved out of stone.

'Let go of me, you—' Rohan was fighting, but he was no match for Daniel's strength.

Over on the hearth the St Bernard began to bark.

'Charles darling,' said Decima, 'did you give George any champagne?'

The noise of the barking seemed to send great shafts through Rachel's consciousness until she began to feel that she was waking at last to reality after a long hypnotized sleep. She stood up suddenly, her feet carrying her around the table to where Rohan was shouting abuse at Daniel, and suddenly it seemed that Daniel didn't exist at all and Rohan was the only one who was real.

'Rohan, you idiot, stop making such a fool of yourself!' Her voice was curt and cold. 'Stop it, do you hear? Stop it!' And when he took no notice of her, she slapped him hard across the mouth.

The crack of the impact of hand against flesh seemed to echo throughout the length of the hall. There was a hideous silence. No one moved. No one spoke. And then Decima yawned and said idly to no one in particular: 'Lord, how tired I am! Goodnight, everyone,' and curled herself up on the hearthrug before one of the fireplaces and went immediately to sleep, her head resting on the St Bernard's massive body as he lay beside her.

'Well,' said old Conor Douglas, the lawyer of Cluny Gualach, rising briskly from the table as if nothing had happened, 'I think we should be on our way, Rosalind.'

'Yes, we too must be going,' said Robert MacDonald for all the world as if the dinner-party had ended with perfect normalcy. 'Thank you so much, Charles, for a most excellent meal.'

'Most delightful . . .'

'We did enjoy ourselves . . .'

'Thank you again for your hospitality . . .'

The endless stream of conversation trickled on with a remorseless inevitability until finally the last goodbye had been said, the front door closed and bolted after the last guest, and Ruthven was alone at last with those who lived within its walls.

Without a word Charles went straight to the library and slammed the door shut behind him.

'Exit Charles,' said Rohan, 'thinly disguised as an insulted English gentleman.' And he laughed.

'Exit Rohan,' said Rachel unsmiling, 'appearing undisguised as a very drunk, very foolish overgrown schoolboy. This way.'

'Which way? Here, take your hand off my arm, Raye! What do you think you're doing?'

'We're going upstairs.'

'But—'

'Don't argue.'

'Yes, but look here—'

'Shut up.'

'What about Decima'

'She's passed out. Daniel and Rebecca will see to her.'

'Oh no,' said Rohan forlornly, 'no, don't leave her with the Careys. Don't leave her with them.'

'Don't be silly.'

Half-way up the stairs he said: 'I'm crazy about her, Raye. I always have been. I never told you.'

'No,' she said. 'You never told me.'

'I'd do anything for her,' he said. 'Anything at all.'

'Yes.'

'I'd marry her but Charles won't give her a divorce.'

'No, I understand he's set on a reconciliation.'

'But at least I made her leave Daniel. She saw that she could trust me more than she could trust him.'

'Yes.'

'Daniel doesn't give a damn for her. I'm the one who really loves her. She knows that now.'

'Yes.'

'She's going to come away with me. She's promised. She's going to be mine for ever and ever and ever . . .'

'Mind the corner. It's dark down here.'

'. . . ever and ever and ever . . .'

They walked on down the south wing past the south-west turret room to the west wing that faced the sea.

'Which is your room, Rohan?'

'This one. No, this one. I can't remember.'

It was the second room. Rachel found the lamp, but he had fallen across the bed in a stupor even before she had managed to light the wick. After pulling off his shoes and arranging the quilt on top of him as best she could, she blew out the lamp again and went back past the south-west turret room to her own room in the south wing. She shut the door in exhaustion, lit the lamp on the table and sank down in the chair before the hearth.

After ten minutes or so she remembered she had left Decima sleeping downstairs. Perhaps she should go and see if she were all right. No, let someone else look after Decima for a change! Decima with her sneering tongue and cool hateful remarks . . . What was it she had said? *You look awful, Raye! What's the matter? Hasn't Daniel given you his best smile today?*

It was an unforgivable taunt to be made in front of a gathering of strangers, and Rachel had no intention of forgiving. Decima could go to the devil as far as she was concerned.

'Don't leave Decima with the Careys!' Rohan had said, maudlin with his surfeit of liquor. 'Don't leave her alone with them . . .'

'I don't trust the Careys,' Decima had said. 'They're against me – everyone's against me – don't let them turn you against me too, Rachel . . .'

All that nonsense about Charles wanting to kill her so that he might inherit Ruthven . . . Absurd. Charles wouldn't kill any-one, although God knows he certainly must have felt like killing Decima when she humiliated him before all his friends . . .

Decima must have drunk a great deal. Normally, as Rachel well knew, she could drink a fair share of Scotch and still show no trace of having drunk more than a glass of iced water. Rohan too was accustomed to liquor. His bachelor life in London had ensured that.

I wonder, thought Rachel, why they both got so drunk. I wonder what made them drink so much.

She wanted desperately to relax and find peace in sleep, but her mind was vibrantly alive, the thoughts milling through her brain, and after a while she stood up and moved restlessly out into the corridor. There was a light glowing beneath Decima's door, and as she drew nearer she could hear the faint sound of a man's voice and a woman's murmur from within.

She knocked softly on the panels. The murmuring ceased at once.

'Who is it?' called Decima sleepily.

'Rachel. I just wondered if you were all right.'

'Yes, thanks. Daniel brought me upstairs a little while ago. There's no need for you to worry.'

Rachel wanted to ask who was with her but was so convinced that it was Daniel that her courage failed her. 'I'll see you to-morrow, then,' she said, turning away. 'Goodnight, Decima.'

' 'Night.' Decima sounded a long way off, barely conscious.

Rachel waited for the murmuring to begin again but it did not. At last, not wanting to risk being found listening outside the door, she walked on to the head of the stairs and glanced down into the hall. The remains of the dinner-party lay hap-hazardly on the long banquet table below and, although the candles had been snuffed, the lamps still burned on the chest and side-tables around the room. The twin fires were now mere glowing embers in the great fireplaces, and Rachel noticed that the St Bernard had left his favourite place on the hearth and was stretched out in slumber before the door of the small drawing-room across the hall.

Rachel went over to the library door and knocked softly. 'Charles?'

There was no reply.

She tried again. 'Charles, it's Rachel. May I come in?'

There was still no reply, but she could see the light shining beneath the door. Perhaps he had fallen asleep. Cautiously she turned the handle, pushed open the door a little way and began to walk into the room.

Her feet stopped just after she had crossed the threshold. Paralysis flickered through her body with lightning speed, tak-ing from her even the power to draw a breath, and then sudden-ly the gasp of shock was tearing at her lungs and her throat was dry as she tried to scream. For Charles lay slumped back in his chair with Rebecca's ivory dagger in his chest and she knew at once, even before she moved forward again towards him, that he was dead.

<h1 style="text-align:center">IV</h1>

She could not bring herself to touch him. He lay there still and silent in death, his face tilted downwards, his arms hanging over the arms of the chair behind the desk, and all she could do was look down at him in horror and try to think what she could do. The white ivory of the dagger gleamed in the lamplight. The carved sheath lay neatly on the windowseat close at hand where the murderer had discarded it.

The murderer. Charles had been murdered.

There was a fire in the grate, the flames flickering so feebly that they were almost moribund. There were papers burning, the trace of scorched dark leather. When she knelt down on the hearth a second later she saw that someone had tried to burn Rebecca's diary in the dying fire a short while ago.

A door slammed somewhere. There were footsteps crossing the hall, getting louder and louder as they drew nearer to the library. Propelled by fears and instincts which she didn't even begin to analyse, Rachel sprang to her feet and stepped swiftly behind the long red curtains which stretched from the floor to the ceiling in front of the french windows.

She was just in time.

She heard the door open even though she didn't dare look to see who had entered, heard the abrupt silence which came the next moment, heard the click of the latch as the door was shut quietly again.

The silence after that seemed to go on and on and on. The only thing she could see was the red velvet of the curtains before her, but she knew just as surely as if she could have seen him face to face that it was Daniel who had entered the room. She could imagine him beside the body, noticing the dagger, seeing the sheath, catching sight of the scorched diary just as she had done.

He was very silent, she thought; it was almost as if he had known what he was going to find . . . But that was impossible, of course.

Or was it?

She heard a small noise then, the crackling of scorched papers, and guessed he must be pulling the diary from the grate. She heard him throw on another log and use the bellows to work up the flames to a blaze which would effectively destroy everything he had been unable to remove.

After that there was another silence. What would he be doing now? Hardly daring to breathe she found the chink in the curtains and glanced through them into the room beyond.

He was wiping the handle of the dagger with his handkerchief. As she watched he picked up the sheath from the table and wiped that too before replacing it again where he had found it. Then, very carefully, he wrapped Charles' fingers around the hilt of the dagger and rearranged the body so that Charles' weight was thrust forward still farther onto the blade in his chest.

She edged farther to the right of the chink in the curtains for safety, and as she shifted her position the curtain rings far above gave a small, almost inaudible squeak of movement as she touched the material in front of her by accident.

She froze.

There was nothing then, nothing at all. She tried to hear his breathing but the room was as silent as a tomb and she could only hear the thump of her heart and the roar of blood in her ears.

She went on waiting, hardly able to breathe. And then, just as she began to think she was safe after all, he flung back the curtains with a quick flick of his wrists and she was staring up into his eyes.

V

'What are you doing here?'

'I wanted to talk to Charles. I came here about a minute ago and then I heard you coming so I hid here.'

'Why?'

'I don't know.'

He stared at her, his eyes wide and dark, and she leant back against the french windows as her strength deserted her and her limbs began to tremble.

'You'd better make up a better story than that to tell the police,' he said after a while. 'It doesn't sound very convincing.'

'Perhaps it would be more convincing,' she heard herself say in a shaking voice, 'if I told them I saw you take your sister's diary from the grate where it lay burning, wipe her fingerprints from the dagger, and rearrange the body to make it seem as if Charles had committed suicide.'

'Rebecca didn't kill him,' he said again flatly.

'Then who did?'

He turned from her abruptly and moved across the room. 'Why, Decima, of course,' he said. 'Who else?' He wrenched open the door. 'You'd better come and help me find her.'

'Decima didn't kill him,' said Rachel.

'Why do you say that?'

Instinct made her say nothing.

'Why do you say that?' repeated Daniel, but she would not answer him.

The St Bernard was at the foot of the staircase, his tail swaying gently, as he followed Daniel up the stairs to the gallery above.

'Shouldn't we get the police?' Rachel said suddenly.

'Yes, we'll have to take the boat into Kyle of Lochalsh. Or maybe Quist can go if we can wake him up. Did you put him to bed?'

'More or less. Shall I go and try to wake him?'

'No, we must find Decima first.'

'Why not Rebecca?'

'Because Decima was Charles' wife,' said Daniel, 'and whether she killed him or not she has the right to be told first of his death.'

Rachel's mind was spinning. The shock made her thoughts jumbled and confused so that all she was aware of thinking was that Charles had been killed and that one of his guests had killed him. It must be Rebecca, she thought. Decima was in her room. Rohan was drunk in his bed. Daniel . . . But where had Daniel been? With Decima in her room? Had she been confessing to him that she had killed Charles and framed Rebecca, and had Daniel then immediately come downstairs to rearrange the scene of the crime so that Rebecca would be cleared? But Decima had been drunk. Decima had been carried upstairs to her room . . . By Daniel.

They were outside the door.

'Decima,' said Daniel in a low voice and knocked on the panels.

There was no answer.

'Decima?' He opened the door slightly and glanced inside. The next moment he was crossing the room swiftly and Rachel was following him across the threshold.

The bed was empty, as empty as the room itself. It was bitterly cold and the lamp was smoking in the draught from the huge window which was flung open as wide as it would go.

Understanding came to Rachel so quickly that she was conscious of neither shock nor horror, only of a dim, unreal surprise. 'My God—'

'Keep back,' said Daniel suddenly, but she was already beside him at the window and staring down through the darkness at Decima's lifeless body on the stone terrace below.

Somewhere far away in the hall, the grandfather clock began to strike midnight.

Decima had died before her twenty-first birthday.

PART TWO: CLUNY SANDS

CHAPTER ONE

I

Afterwards, all Rachel had wanted to do was to bury herself in the midst of some teeming civilization. She was obsessed with the desire for traffic and huge buildings and throngs of people, some foreign city far south of Ruthven where the sun would scorch the concrete pavements and burn out the memory of silky mists and soft sea breezes. Even London, six hundred miles from those grey stone walls, eventually seemed too close, and even though Daniel was by that time far away in Africa the memory of him lingered with each memory of Ruthven.

She thought of Ruthven often. She knew she would never forget that moment at midnight when she had faced Daniel in Decima's room.

'Can't you see?' he had said to her by that open window with the damp night air chilling the room. 'I've just rearranged Charles' body to look as if he deliberately pressed forward on that dagger and killed himself. The police are going to think he murdered Decima – God knows he had enough provocation after the way she behaved tonight – and then committed suicide. If they think that, there'll be no repercussions for the rest of us. They've got to think that Charles killed Decima and then himself.'

She had stared at him, trying to read his mind and decipher the meaning which lay behind what he had said. After a while she had said, shaken: 'But how can we say that? I spoke to Decima on my way down to the library to find Charles. Her door was closed but I called out from the passage to ask if she was all right and she said she was. Charles died before she did.

'But no one else knows that,' he had said. 'Just you and I. We know that Decima killed Charles and framed it to look as if Rebecca had killed him, but nobody knows that except you and I.'

She had hesitated a long time. She thought of Charles, the evidence that Rebecca had killed him, the proof that Daniel had been so quick to destroy. Daniel must have killed Decima too, unless Daniel himself ... Every muscle in Rachel's body tightened in an agony of nervousness and suspense.

'Don't you understand?' he had said very deliberately. 'It's the easiest way out. All you would have to do would be to omit any mention of the fact that you spoke to Decima before you found Charles dead, and omit all mention of the fact that you saw me rearrange the body. Then once the police accept that explanation, the rest of us won't come under suspicion.'

And still she had hesitated, torn between fear and doubt, knowing what she should do yet not knowing whether she had the strength to do it. At last he had said without emphasis: 'The police could suspect you, you know. If they thought that you were jealous of Decima, that you hated her because she humiliated you, they might think you killed her. They might think Decima had killed Charles and then you killed Decima.'

He had wanted to ensure her silence, her acquiescence in his desire to suppress the truth. She wondered if he had ever realized that even after their quarrel and his rejection of her she would still have done anything to protect him.

'I think I understand,' she had heard herself say at last, her voice seeming strained and distant in her ears. 'Yes, we'd better do as you suggest.'

So she had committed herself and after that there could be no turning back. He had not seemed grateful, she noticed, but only infinitely relieved, as if he had somehow managed to overcome some insuperable obstacle threatening his own security.

The local police had been slow and rustic; when the CID men arrived later, they had found the trail cold and the case a formality. At the ensuing inquest the coroner had been a retired doctor from Fort William, the jury mostly fishermen from Kyle of Lochalsh, and it had seemed obvious to all of them after hearing evidence from the dinner-party guests that Charles had killed his wife and then in despair committed suicide. The papers had made a great splash of it for a couple of days on the front pages, and Charles had had his obituary in *The Times*, but after that the case had been soon forgotten, dismissed as one of the more newsworthy tragedies of the year, and the press had passed to other matters to feed to their voracious readers.

As Decima had died before attaining twenty-one, Charles should have inherited Ruthven under the terms of her father's will, but since by law a murderer cannot profit from his crime, it was held that the estate would revert to Decima's next-of-kin. Since Decima was an orphan with no relatives, this in fact meant that the house and estate of Ruthven passed into the hands of the Crown. The profitable forestry estates were sold to the Forestry Commission, and the house, which no estate agent had been able to sell, was in the end left to fall gradually into decay. As for Willie the gamekeeper and his wife, they had accepted a post on a large estate farther south near Lochaber and when they moved from Ruthven some two months after the inquest they had taken George, the St Bernard, with them.

The incident was closed; the nightmare was over. Rohan, Rachel, Rebecca and Daniel went their separate ways.

For a short time Rachel had stayed in London, not really wanting to leave it, for she loved the city better than any other, and then one day she had met Rebecca by chance in Mayfair. She was teaching, Rachel discovered, lecturing in economics. And Daniel? Yes, he was happy. He had gone out to Africa to teach English and English history in one of the new African states. He seemed to have found his vocation, for apparently he wanted nothing except to remain in the new life he had chosen for himself.

It was then that Rachel realized how empty England was, how unbearably dreary her life had become. The longing to escape became an obsession. She felt she could only begin to live again if she were in a new country, in new surroundings and among new people, and finally she made the decision to go to America where, she had heard, English secretaries were in great demand. She arrived in New York three months later, found a job without difficulty, and quickly made friends at the women's hotel where she was staying. Soon she was sharing a luxury apartment with three other girls in midtown Manhattan just west of Fifth Avenue, and four years later was surprised to look back and find how quickly the time had passed.

It was then that Rohan arrived. He had been working in England for an automobile concern, and now wrote to say that he was to be transferred to his firm's New York branch. He had, he disclosed, requested the transfer.

She met him at the airport. It was rather absurd because she felt like crying at the sight of someone from home, and he, emotional as ever, was obviously overcome with pleasure at seeing her again. He looked tired after the journey, but his grey eyes were as brilliant as ever and his hair, still straw-coloured, rose up in a tuft above his forehead where he had pulled it in his excitement.

In the cab on the way back into the city she said: 'But I still don't understand why you requested the transfer.'

'Maybe for the same reasons as the ones which persuaded you to leave England,' he answered, staring out of the window at the approaching skyline of Manhattan. 'And I'm not as English as most Englishmen. There's a lot of foreign blood in me. I didn't think I would find it hard to live abroad for a while.'

'It's funny,' she said. 'I don't know why, but I half thought you might be getting interested in Rebecca. When you wrote to tell me you were coming to the States I thought you were writing to tell me you were engaged. You mentioned her quite often in your letters.'

'I saw a little of her now and then,' he said, very casual, almost uninterested. 'It was nice, but . . . she wasn't really my type. And besides—' He stopped.

'Besides?'

He turned towards her and she saw that his face, usually so mobile and expressive, was very still.

'There were too many memories,' he said. 'For both of us. It was better to go our separate ways.'

She nodded silently, making no comment. It was the one and only reference that either of them made to Ruthven, and it was never mentioned between them again.

Yet still she thought of Daniel.

Daniel in Africa, Daniel abandoning career and home and country to teach African children in a gesture which was as out of character as it was striking. She could never understand what had taken him to Africa, for Daniel was not the kind of man who offered his services to welfare organizations for a nominal salary, and still less the kind of man who would feel any desire to teach children in a new country with poor facilities. With his background of scholarship he might have ultimately attained all the academic honours he could have wished for; she could see him so clearly at Cambridge with its ancient beautiful buildings, visualize him so easily accepting a good academic post and lecturing to brilliant gifted students; there would have been a professorship waiting in the future, a successful business and social life, a life in England among English people in an English university town.

But he had turned his back on all that. The absoluteness of the gesture with its sweeping implications was something she could understand, even if she did not understand the gesture itself. Daniel had always seemed so vivid and positive to her that she could easily imagine him reaching a decision to change his entire life and then having the courage to keep to his decision and follow it through to its conclusion. That at least was in character. But to go to Africa, to seek the steamy torrid climate of the Equator, to bury himself as an obscure teacher far from home was a decision which seemed both bewildering and bizarre.

She wanted to talk to Rohan about it, but Rohan was always so scrupulously careful never to mention the subject of Ruthven now that they were so far from the past that she never managed to broach the subject with him. Rohan quickly settled down in the city, soon gathered a host of friends around him, and before long he was again the leader of the crowd, just as he had been long ago, as far back as she could remember, and after a while she began to feel that her life had swung back to normal again after some nightmare deviation from its appointed course.

But all she was aware of thinking whenever she met another man was: he is nothing compared to Daniel.

Her mother wrote to her from England: 'So you're meeting

such a lot of people, dear. It must be lovely to have Rohan there with you. Is there anyone special at the moment? It's so amazing to think that next September you'll be twenty-eight. . . .'

Her mother was thinking of tomorrow, and tomorrow for Rachel did not exist. Tomorrow was a great emptiness, a desert stretching into nothingness before the oasis of today, and the landscape was so desolate that she did not even dare to look at it.

I shall never marry, she thought. Not while Daniel's image is still so strong in my mind.

But Daniel had preferred his life to take a different course. He had never loved her, just as she had never really loved him, and she could see now that her whole attitude to him was a romantic attachment, a young girl's infatuation which she had never fully outgrown; it was surely best to pretend even to herself that the whole episode was already forgotten, and then perhaps she would find it easier to obliterate him from her mind for all time.

It was evening. She was going out to dinner and had just had a bath. There was a long mirror in the living-room next to the desk, and she had always sat in front of it to put on her make-up because the light from the desk lamp was perfect for applying cosmetics. As she began to put on her make-up the phone on the desk started to ring.

She picked up the receiver without interest. 'Hullo?'

'Rachel,' said Rohan, and his voice sounded thin and far away as if he were speaking from a great distance. 'I had to call you.'

Rohan was always dramatic. His reason for calling was probably trivial.

'I'm just going out,' she said. 'Can I call you back later?'

'No,' he said, 'no, I have to tell you. I had a letter from England today.'

She thought she heard his voice tremble. Her fingers suddenly tightened on the receiver. 'From England?'

'From Rebecca, Rachel. From Rebecca Carey.'

She could see her expression in the long mirror, watch the

colour ebb from her face. It was as if she were watching a film, seeing a stranger whom she did not know.

'I got the letter this morning,' he was saying. 'I couldn't think why she was writing, as we only exchanged addresses as a formality.'

'What did she say?'

'Can't you guess? It's Daniel, Rachel – Daniel's returning from Africa, coming back into our lives . . .'

II

Daniel had often asked himself why he had gone abroad. He, who had always lived his life in the most English of environments, who had lived in the oldest and most English parts of England, who had worked in such a peculiarly English world of academic research – why should he of all people have suddenly decided to turn his back on it all and try instead to teach in a hostile foreign land for little money and little prestige? He had gone back to Cambridge after Ruthven fully prepared to resume his life where he had left it, to pick up the threads as if he had never been away and to slip back with ease into the intellectual satisfaction of his work and his life amongst those ancient, beautiful surroundings. He had never anticipated what had happened when he went back. He had never once thought that the world he loved would have changed so that it seemed to him yet another Ruthven in its arid, desolate sterility; he could never once have imagined that he would ever pause on the Bridge of Sighs and look at the smooth waters of the Cam below and think to himself: 'I have no place here any more. I'm a stranger knocking on the door and trying to gain entrance, but I've come to the wrong door. There's nothing here for me.'

His work suddenly seemed a mere mechanical exercise of his brain, and even his ambition had died. He had waited, hoping his apathy was some form of reaction from the events at Ruthven, but the state of mind persisted and at last he realized clearly that he had to get away – away from Cambridge, away from England, and most of all away from Rebecca. It was true they had never spoken of Ruthven, and Rebecca had shied away from all mention of Charles and Decima, but Daniel, convinced as he was that she had killed them both in a burst of frenzied rage and revenge, found it impossible to be at ease with her. Several times he tried to force himself to speak of it to her, but each time he had failed. She must know, he thought, that he had covered up for her; she must realize that he knew . . . But if she did, she seemed determined not to speak of it, and the awkwardness between them became more pronounced. When he had decided to go abroad she was very distressed and for a time tried to persuade him to stay, but when she saw he was determined she gave up her attempts at persuasion and appeared resigned to the situation.

A voluntary educational organization had seized on the opportunity to enlist a graduate capable of teaching English; within three months he had a class of forty African children in Accra and was learning to live in the country which had once been called the White Man's Grave.

He found he enjoyed teaching more than he thought he would, and, contrary to what he had always imagined, the younger his pupils were the more he enjoyed teaching them. *When I eventually return to England,* he thought, *this is what I shall do. I'll get a school of my own and teach young children, not vegetate in some great university lecturing to pseudo adults who think they're God's gift to society.*

The decision pleased him; he was happy. Perhaps he would even have stayed longer in Accra if he had not begun to think more and more of Rachel Lord.

He didn't know why he thought of her so often. Perhaps it was because he had never really been able to make up his mind about her. She had seemed so full of candour and sincerity, so honest and unspoilt and unsophisticated, that it had sickened him to discover she had stooped to spying and telling tales in the violence of her jealousy of him. And then later . . . It was Rohan, Rachel had said, I never told Charles. It was Rohan . . .

But Decima had said Rachel was the one who had told Charles. 'Can't you see she's beside herself with jealousy?' she had blazed to Daniel. 'Can't you see she has this schoolgirl crush on you and is as jealous as hell?'

He had never even considered that it might be Quist, and yet it was much more likely that Quist would have been the one to cause trouble. But why had Decima lied? Because it was *she* who was jealous, *she* who was spiteful enough to want to hurt Rachel and pay her back for capturing Daniel's attention? Perhaps after all Rachel had been speaking the truth, and if so perhaps she was still everything he had first imagined her to be. The more he considered the situation, the more convinced he became that he had misjudged her, and the more he became convinced that he had judged her wrongly the more he wanted to see her. Now, five years after he had left England, he found he was thinking of her all the time. He thought of her when his students asked him questions about English places and English people; he thought of her whenever he received his three-week-old copy of the *Sunday Times* and saw the theatre news and the book reviews; he thought of her when he was introduced to other women and above all he thought of her each year on the anniversary of those terrible days at Ruthven when he relived the memories he would carry with him to the end of his life. Sometimes it seemed to him that he would only have to close his eyes to be back again at Ruthven and facing her beside the open window of Decima's room.

He was not sure when it first became clear to him that he would have to see her again. Perhaps the turning point came when he received a letter from his sister mentioning that she had met Rohan Quist again by chance in London and that he was about to leave England to work in New York.

'Apparently Rachel is working in New York already,' Rebecca had written, 'so I suppose this will give them the opportunity to revive their platonic friendship again.'

It was then that he had started to wonder whether Quist and Rachel would ever discuss Ruthven when they met. Unless Rachel was very careful such a discussion could be extremely dangerous.

He thought about it for a long time, remembering every detail of those last hours at Ruthven, but the more he thought about it the less convinced he was that everything was perfectly safe. Supposing Rachel betrayed to Quist that she knew the coroner's verdict had been wrong . . . Quist had loved Decima. Suppose he got it into his head to resurrect the entire business. . . .

It was then that Daniel first conceived the idea of seeing Rachel again to warn her not to talk, and once the idea of seeing her was in his mind there was no putting it aside.

Several of Rebecca's letters had referred to Quist after that first meeting when he had told her he was planning to join Rachel in New York.

'Rohan rang up,' she had written in the next letter, 'and asked me out to dinner. I nearly refused and then I thought; hell, why not? So I went. We went to an extremely good restaurant, and much to my surprise I rather enjoyed myself. He seems to have matured a great deal and it was hard to believe he was the same person as the Rohan Quist we knew at Ruthven . . . He didn't refer to Ruthven at all, or to Charles or Decima, but for me at any rate, if not for him, the memories were there like a great wall between us. . . .'

Rohan had taken her out several times after that. Then later she had written:

'Saw Rohan again last night. It was his birthday and he said he wanted to go out and have a few drinks somewhere, so we went to the Dorchester and got rather tight on vodka martinis. After the fourth he started to talk about Rachel, and by the time he had finished the fifth he was talking of Ruthven. "It's a funny thing, he said, "but I'm sure Rachel knows something." And I said: "Knows what?"

' "About Ruthven," he said. "She won't talk about it, though. She never talks of Ruthven. But I'm sure she knows something."

'I said: "Why do you say that?"

'And he said: "Because I've known Rachel over twenty-five years and I know her better than most men know their own sisters. I know when she's keeping her mouth shut and when she isn't."

'Well, I couldn't resist it – I just had to ask him if he hadn't always been a little in love with her. And he said: "A little perhaps." I thought he was going to say more but when he didn't I asked him why he didn't marry her.

'He just laughed. He was very drunk. Then he said suddenly: "Maybe I will! It's about time I got married." and he laughed again suddenly, as if he'd been very clever, and he went on laughing until he knocked over his glass . . . We went soon after that. He said he'd phone me before he left for New York next week, but somehow I doubt if he will."

Rebecca had been correct. Rohan had never phoned.

It was soon after that letter that Daniel had begun to make arrangements for his departure. It was impossible to leave at once, for the summer term was just beginning and he was bound to stay until it was finished, but just over three months later he said goodbye to his students in Accra, boarded the plane for London and began his long, dangerous journey back into the past.

III

All Rachel could think of was that Daniel was coming. After Rohan had told her the news and had said he would come round to her apartment straight away, she hadn't moved from her position in front of the mirror for a long time, and then at last she picked up the receiver of the phone again and cancelled her date for the evening.

Daniel was coming. It had been five years since Ruthven but now the five years were as if they had never existed at all. Daniel had left Africa and was already in London on his way back into their lives.

'Rebecca said in her letter that he wanted to see you,' Rohan had said to her over the phone. 'I don't understand it at all. You haven't been in touch with him, have you?'

And she had said blankly: 'Of course not.'

'Then why does he want to see you?'

'I – don't know.'

There was a long silence. Then:

'I'll come round right away,' Rohan had said abruptly, and hung up.

Daniel was coming. He wanted to see her. Why else would he want to see her unless it was because of Ruthven?

She saw the house then so clearly in her mind that it seemed to her that she would only have to close her eyes to be back there again breathing the damp pure air and feeling the soft sea breeze moist against her cheek. She saw the bare stretches of the moors ending in the dark lines of the forestry plantation, the desolate mountains, the swaying sea, and there before her eyes were the turrets and towers of Ruthven with their grey walls and blank windows.

Her thoughts, as if liberated at last after five years of constant suppression, went on and on and on. She was recalling each detail of her stay five years ago, reliving the horror of those last hours, the discovery of Charles' body, the realization of Decima's death, the agreement she had reached with Daniel . . .

Daniel. Daniel wanted to see her. Daniel was coming to New York.

When Rohan arrived a few minutes later she could hardly reach the door fast enough to answer the bell.

'We'd better go out, hadn't we?' he said as she let him in. 'There's no privacy here.'

'The others are out. They won't be back for hours yet.'

'Okay, then we'll stay here. Let me get you a drink.'

She asked for a Tom Collins and went into the kitchen to fetch the soda from the refrigerator. Later, when he had mixed the drinks, they sat down together on the couch and he gave her a cigarette. After a moment he said with wry cynicism:

'Perhaps he's coming to propose.'

'Oh, for God's sake, Rohan!' She was too tense to laugh at such a preposterous suggestion. 'You know as well as I do that whatever relationship existed between Daniel and me certainly wasn't on that plane. I don't know why he can possibly want to see me, least of all now, five years after Ruthven.'

There was a silence. Rohan leant forward to flick ash into the tray on the table and the light glinted for a moment on the gold of his cuff-links and the crisp white cuff of his shirt below the sleeve of his suit. He looked well dressed and elegant, and the years had smoothed out the angular thinness of his face and body so that all impression of immaturity had been eliminated from his appearance. His fair hair, which had never lost the shining brightness of childhood, was neat and well cut, his fine eyes reflecting the thoughts of his mind like an opaque mirror. She wondered again why he had never married. Perhaps he had always been too conscious of Decima's memory, just as she herself had always been too quick to remember Daniel . . .

'Raye?'

She suddenly realized he had asked her a question. 'I'm sorry,' she said confused. 'I was thinking of something else. What did you say?'

'I was just asking,' said Rohan, 'if you were quite sure you had no idea why Daniel should be looking for you?'

'What do you mean?'

'It's about Ruthven, isn't it?'

'Honestly, Rohan, I—'

'You shielded him, didn't you?'

There was a dead silence. They looked at one another. Then:

'Shielded him?' said Rachel.

'I always suspected you were keeping something back at the inquest. It had to do with Daniel, hadn't it? There was no one else you would have shielded.'

She didn't answer.

'Was Daniel involved?'

She still didn't answer.

'Raye—'

'It was as they said at the inquest,' she interrupted quickly, a spot of colour flaming in each cheek. 'Charles killed Decima and then committed suicide.'

'Yes,' said Rohan. 'Very convenient.' He watched his cigarette burn for a moment. Then suddenly his eyes were looking straight into hers and she knew at once what he was going to say. 'Did Daniel kill Decima?'

'Rohan—'

'He had a good enough motive. She told me on the eve of her birthday that she had originally wanted him to take her away with him, but he had lost interest in her and refused. She was furious with him and determined to pay him back. "I'll make

141

trouble for him," she said to me, "I'll see he doesn't get that post he wants at Cambridge." She was full of plans to ruin him. Did he kill her?'

'I—' The horror of those last hours at Ruthven made speech difficult. 'I – don't know,' she said desperately at last. 'I just don't know, Rohan. He had the opportunity. He was in Decima's room talking to her before I went down to the library to find Charles.'

'He was *where*?'

'In Decima's room. I knocked on her door to ask her if she was all right and she said she was. Someone else was with her at the time because I could hear the murmur of voices—'

'You mean,' said Rohan slowly, 'that Decima was alive then?'

'Yes. Yes, she was alive.'

'But that means—'

'I know. Charles didn't kill Decima. He was the one who died first.'

'But my God, Raye, why on earth didn't you tell the police?'

'It was the easiest way out, Rohan . . .' She told him about Charles then, described how Daniel had destroyed the evidence that Rebecca had committed the murder. 'He said it was obvious that Decima had killed Charles—'

'Obvious?' said Rohan amazed. 'Obvious? Why the hell should Decima have killed Charles? I talked to her that evening! She was full of plans for getting a divorce – I had offered to take her away with me for a while – we had planned to leave Ruthven together the next day. That was why we both got drunk – we were drunk with exhilaration and pleasure! Why should she have murdered Charles? She didn't need to! Isn't it much more obvious that Rebecca killed him? She was out of her mind with frustration and rage. She could easily have killed him in a fit of fury and left Daniel to clear up after her! That to me is much more plausible than to suggest that Decima was the murderess.'

'Daniel said Rebecca had been framed.'

'Well, of course he'd say that! Of course!'

'But Decima – who pushed her from the window?'

'Why, Daniel, of course! Who else? When Rebecca came and

told him what had happened, he suddenly saw how he could use the situation to his best advantage. If he were to silence Decima he could make it seem that Charles had killed his wife and then committed suicide. In that way he would extricate Rebecca from a very unpleasant situation and also eliminate the threat Decima presented to his future and prospects. So he went back to Decima's room – which he must have left shortly after you spoke to Decima on your way down to the library – killed her, and then returned to the library to rearrange the body and obliterate all trace of Rebecca from the scene of the crime. Imagine how he must have felt when he found you there! His one chance lay in the fact that you were sufficiently – that you cared for him enough to agree to shield him, so he told you what to tell the police, and gambled on the likelihood that you would do as he said.'

Rachel ground her cigarette to ashes, stood up and moved restlessly over to the window.

There was another long silence.

'Why on earth didn't you tell me this before, Raye?'

What was there to say? That she had never been able to acknowledge to herself the probability of Daniel's guilt? That even after five years she was still in love with the memory of a man who had never loved her in return? There was no logical answer, no easy explanation. 'It seemed the simplest way out at the time,' she heard herself say at last. 'I know it was weak and stupid of me, but it was such a temptation to do as he suggested and make the inquest a simple uncomplicated affair. I'd reached the end of the road by that time – I couldn't have endured more police investigations or the possibility of being detained at Ruthven any longer. I just wanted to leave, to forget, to escape.'

'It might have seemed the simplest way out at the time,' Rohan said, 'but I doubt if it's going to be quite so simple now. You realize of course why Daniel's coming to look for you.'

She stared at him blankly.

'He's heard through Rebecca that I'm in New York. He realizes that I'll be seeing you constantly. He thinks you're

143

going to talk, Rachel – he thinks that in the end you'll tell me the truth. You're a menace to his security.'

The silence then was so acute that it seemed almost audible. The large, softly lit room seemed poised and waiting, and as Rachel stood beside the long mirror and caught sight of her reflection it was as if she saw a stranger with whom she had no connexion, a girl with wide, blank grey eyes in a white frozen face.

'What shall I do?' she said, and suddenly the years fell away and she was a child again turning to Rohan for comfort and advice. 'What shall I do?'

He got up, crossed the room and paused very close to her so that they were a mere few inches apart. 'You don't have to worry,' he said softly. 'You don't have to worry about any-thing. I'll look after you.' And he took her in his arms.

At first she was so surprised that she had no reaction at all and then she felt a surge of gratitude and a wave of overwhelm-ing relief. Tears pricked her eyes. She slipped her arms around his waist and pressed her face against his shoulder, and present-ly she felt his lips brush her hair and touch her forehead. She raised her face to his. 'What shall we do?'

'We'll leave New York. I'll say I have to go home for a few days for family reasons – I'm more or less my own boss at work, so no one's going to ask any questions. You'll have to leave your job – or take some unpaid leave. One or the other. Is your passport in order? We'll leave New York tomorrow evening.'

'Supposing Daniel should arrive before then?'

'He doesn't know where you live – he only knows my address through Rebecca. His only way of contacting you will be by first contacting me, and I can stall him off. You're safe for a time, anyway. Have you got enough money for your fare?'

'Yes, I think so.'

'I'll ring up and make the reservations.' His hand was already on the phone. 'We'll try and get on a flight tomorrow evening.'

'Rohan—'

'Yes?'

'Suppose he follows us? Where shall we go when we get to England?'

'Somewhere remote and isolated, where we can set a trap for him. Of course! The obvious place! Why didn't I think of it before? We'll go back to Ruthven . . .'

IV

Rebecca was at the airport to meet him as the plane from Accra finally touched down on British soil. After the long tedious minutes spent in Customs and Immigration, he passed through the barrier to join her and she was running into his arms.

'Danny . . . oh, Danny . . .' She was hugging him fiercely as if to make up for the five years he had spent away from her, and he pressed her to him tightly in response. Presently she looked up at him with shining eyes and they laughed together in happiness.

'How tanned you are!' she exclaimed. 'You look so well . . . Oh Danny, how wonderful to see you again . . .'

She had her car, a small Mini-Morris, parked outside the building and after they had all his luggage safely stowed away they set off to her tiny flat in Bayswater. They were just turning off the main road into Hammersmith some time later when she asked him the inevitable question.

'What are you going to do now, Danny? Have you any ideas?'

'Yes,' he said without hesitation, his eyes on the road ahead. 'I have a flight to New York booked on Monday. I'm going to spend a week or two in America.'

He heard her gasp, saw her hands swerve on the wheel. 'America?' she said incredulously, as if she could hardly believe her ears. 'New York?'

'I plan to go to the Embassy tomorrow to get a visa.'

After a moment she said: 'Why?'

He made no reply.

'It's not because of Rachel and Rohan, is it?'

He stared straight ahead of him, vaguely aware of all the changes in the Hammersmith he remembered, savouring the English roads and the English houses and the signposts bearing English names.

145

'If it is,' she said, 'you can save yourself a plane fare. They're back in England.'

The landscape froze before his eyes. He whirled to face her. 'They're back?'

'I was going to tell you—'

'Where are they?'

'Rohan called me yesterday morning soon after they'd arrived. He said they were over here for two weeks' holiday and were on their way north to Scotland.'

He stared at her incredulously. 'You didn't tell him, did you, that I was coming home?'

The car swerved again; she drew into the side of the road and switched off the engine. The traffic roared past.

'Well, yes,' she said. 'I did. I wrote and told him last week soon after you'd told me your decision.' She hesitated uneasily. Then: 'I'm sorry, Danny. I didn't realize—'

'It doesn't matter. It's done now. It was my fault for not anticipating that you'd tell him.' He switched on the engine again for her and pressed the starter. 'Don't let's stop here.'

'But I don't understand,' said Rebecca bewildered, slipping the car into gear and easing out the clutch. 'What do you want with them, Danny? Why do you want to see them now after all this time?'

'It's just something I have to straighten out with Rachel,' he said, and his mouth was dry as he spoke. 'I'd rather not go into details. Whereabouts in Scotland are they going?'

'To Kyle of Lochalsh,' said Rebecca. 'Rohan said they were planning to visit Ruthven.'

V

They had taken the night train from London to Edinburgh and had just had lunch on Princes Street by a window which faced the castle. They had already hired a car for a week at one of the local garages and were planning to set off after lunch on the north journey into the Highlands towards Fort William, Inverness and Kyle of Lochalsh. The sun was shining. Outside, the gardens at the foot of the castle were immensely green and the grey castle walls, standing aloft on the black upthrust of volcanic rock, shimmered in the heat haze.

'I still don't see how meeting Daniel at Ruthven will ever induce him to admit anything,' Rachel was saying as the waitress brought them coffee.

'He'll have to admit something,' Rohan said dryly. 'He won't follow us all the way to Ruthven for the purpose of keeping his mouth shut.'

'But why couldn't we have met him in London?'

'Because he's more likely to take risks and give himself away in a remote place. In London he'd be too much on his guard.'

'Do you think so? I still can't help wishing we didn't have to go back.'

'Look,' said Rohan, 'who's in charge of this plan – you or me? Right. Well, sooner or later Daniel's going to catch up with you and if he's going to catch up with you, it's best for me to be there too, isn't it? Right. Well, assuming that I'll have to face a potentially dangerous man and deal with him in whatever way the situation demands, I think I have the right to choose a location. And I chose Ruthven.'

'Yes, said Rachel. 'All right.'

He capitulated at once. 'Look, Raye, I'm sorry – I didn't mean to upset you – I know it's all the most awful strain for you—'

'No,' she said. 'It's all right. Really, Rohan, it's all right.'

They drank their coffee. Then:

'Rohan.'

'Yes?'

'You're not going to kill him, are you?'

'Not unless I have to,' said Rohan, 'but if he tries to harm you I'll break every bone in his body without any hesitation at all.'

'Is that why you have brought the gun?'

'Well, I have to have some protection, don't I? Besides, he may well be armed himself.'

'Yes, said Rachel. 'I suppose he might.'

147

Rohan's hand slid across the table and closed on hers. 'You're not still in love with him, are you?'

'No, of course not. That's all over and done with and has been for five years.'

He went on holding her hand beneath his own. After a while he said: 'How much longer do we have to go on pretending to ourselves that we're just good friends?'

She looked up. The sun was slanting right through the window into her eyes and he saw her expression of astonishment before she leaned forward out of the shaft of light and put her face in shadow. 'I'm not sure,' she said at last, 'that I quite understand you.'

'No?' he said. 'It's very simple. Now that I know for certain that you've got over this feeling you had for Daniel, I was wondering if you'd marry me.'

She was silent for a long time, looking into his eyes. In the end she looked away. Her face was grave and still, and it was impossible to tell what she was thinking, but he knew instinctively that she was going to refuse.

'Do you intend to remain unmarried all your life?' he heard himself say quickly. 'We know each other so well, Rachel – we can relax and feel at ease with each other, we suit each other so well. Why go on as we have been doing in an endless attempt to find someone else? I would have asked you before if I hadn't thought you were still emotionally involved with Daniel. I've known for a long while that you're the woman I want to marry.'

'No,' she said. 'I'm just the *kind* of woman you want to marry. It's not the same thing.'

'You don't understand—'

'You don't love me, Rohan! Well, yes, perhaps you do in your own way, but not in a way a husband loves his wife.'

'You're a perfectionist,' he said. 'You're waiting for a glamorised, unreal brand of love which doesn't really exist. You'll wait for ever, Rachel, can't you see? You'll wait for ever for the kind of love that doesn't exist outside the pages of romantic fiction!'

'I'd rather wait for ever,' she said deliberately, 'than marry a man I only half-loved.' And then instantly: 'Rohan, it's not because I care nothing for you – I do care a great deal, you know I do – but surely you must see that we wouldn't be suited, that marriage wouldn't really work . . . I'm sorry.' She fumbled with her handbag, almost knocked over her coffee cup. 'Shall we go? There are people over there waiting for tables . . .'

He rose without a word, helped her on with her coat and then went to the cashier's desk to pay the bill.

'I'm sorry, Rohan,' she said again as they went out into the street. 'Please forgive me—'

'There's nothing to forgive.' He smiled at her. 'If you have such qualms about the subject we'd do better not to marry. But in case you should change your mind, the offer still stands.'

They walked down Princes Street, turned up the road where they had left the car. Rachel's mind was in such turmoil that she scarcely knew where she was going. Rohan's proposal had caught her completely unawares and her thoughts, already confused over Daniel, were whirled into greater bewilderment and chaos than ever before. She had answered Rohan instinctively, but even now her logic was beginning to question her instinct. Every reason which Rohan had put forward for marriage was sound; there was every likelihood that they would be as happily married as most couples; he cared for her enough to be with her now when she needed him most of all, and he was always the first person she turned to; she was nearly twenty-eight years old and could certainly do far worse than marry Rohan who at thirty-one was successful in his work, popular with his friends, and good-looking in his own unusual way.

Why, then, had she refused his offer so quickly that her reaction was almost an automatic reflex of her mind?

The answer came straight away, flashing across her thoughts before she could even struggle to suppress it, and she knew well enough why she had rejected Rohan.

He was nothing compared to Daniel.

VI

Daniel and Rebecca had discussed Ruthven in great detail for some time. The subject, unmentioned between them for so long, proved to be so enlightening to both of them that they had recalled with meticulous precision each incident and scene which had preceded the murders. Afterwards Daniel felt so exhausted that he had a bath and slept for a couple of hours before shaving and getting dressed. It was evening, and from the noises in the kitchen he guessed that Rebecca was cooking a meal for them. He picked up the receiver and phoned London Airport.

'When's the next flight to Inverness, please?'

'One moment, sir.'

His call was switched to another extension. There was a click, another voice, and he had to repeat his question.

'The next flight leaves at ten o'clock tonight, sir.'

'Is there a vacancy on it?'

'For how many?'

'Just one.'

'One moment.' Another click, a buzz, a few seconds of empty silence. Then: 'Yes, we have a cancellation so there's a seat available. Would you—'

'Yes,' said Daniel. 'I'll take it. My name is Carey. What time should I be at the airport and where can I pick up my ticket?'

Rebecca had come out of the kitchen but he scarcely noticed her. Then: 'Thank you,' he said, and hung up the receiver.

'Danny—'

'I'm sorry,' he said to her. 'But I really have to go. I shan't be away long, only for a couple of days or so. I'll explain all about it when I get back.'

'Do you want me to come with you?' She was fighting to overcome her disappointment at the thought of losing him so soon. 'Can I help at all?'

'No,' he said, 'this is something which has to be settled between Quist, Rachel and myself. You stay here. I'll be all right – I know exactly what I'm doing . . .'

Rachel and Rohan did not know that while they were spending the night at Kyle of Lochalsh Daniel was sleeping in a hotel at Inverness. They had arrived after dark and found rooms in one of the small hotels near the harbour. After a late supper they had gone to bed and slept until it was time for breakfast at nine o'clock the next morning.

The weather was as unexpectedly fine as it had been in Edinburgh the previous day. Rachel woke to find the sun sparkling on the harbour and glittering on the array of boats moored along the quay. Across the sea loomed the distant heights of Skye and the gulls wheeled and mewed over the stone houses of the town around her. Once she was dressed she paused by the window again to survey the scene, and then Rohan was knocking on her door and they went downstairs to breakfast together.

'How did you sleep?' said Rohan over the toast and marmalade.

'Surprisingly well. I suppose I was very tired after the journey.'

'Yes, I was too.'

They ate for a moment in silence. Then: 'I'll ask the landlord where we can hire a boat from,' Rohan said. 'There shouldn't be any difficulty in getting one.'

'No, I shouldn't think so,' said Rachel, and felt a small core of fear harden noticeably inside her.

She was dreading the return to Ruthven. It had been bad enough returning to Kyle of Lochalsh with its memories of shopping with Decima and the meeting with Daniel in the wheelhouse, but the very idea of seeing Ruthven again was almost more than she could bear. Closing her mind against it resolutely, she poured herself another cup of tea and helped herself to an additional slice of toast, but her nervousness was soon so immense that she had to leave both unfinished.

'Ready?' said Rohan at last. 'Then let's go.'

It took them about an hour to find the type of boat they

wanted. Then after they had stocked the small galley with provisions of all kinds, they cast off from the quay and headed out to sea.

They lost sight of the town less than twenty minutes later.

The wave of isolation that hit Rachel then was so immense that she scarcely knew how to control it. She left the deck and shut herself in the galley below in the hope that she would be able to block out her fear if she didn't see the increasing bleakness of the landscape and the appalling loneliness of those barren shores, but the fear persisted and in the end she drank a double Scotch to steady her nerves. After that she felt better. She had another, to be quite safe, and then went back on deck to join Rohan in the wheelhouse.

'How are we doing?'

'Pretty well. It's a beautiful day, isn't it? I've never seen the sea so calm here before.'

The boat sped on through the dark blue waters, and the landscape, basking in the unaccustomed sunshine, seemed to have lost its quality of overwhelming desolation and become breathtaking in its stark magnificence. Rachel found she could look at it now without feeling fear or dread, and when, at last, she saw the promontory which would bring them to Ruthven, she felt her nerves sharpen again in anticipation.

'Isn't it odd?' said Rohan, and she knew then that he too was uneasy. 'It's just as if nothing had changed. It's hard to realize that Charles and Decima aren't waiting to meet us and that Mrs Willie isn't baking bread in the kitchen and that George isn't snoozing before the fire in the hall.'

They rounded the promontory. There was a shower of spray as the boat met a complex of currents, and then they were heading directly inland and Ruthven lay before them across the water. The sun shone on the grey walls and made the background of mountains and moors shimmer in a green-purple haze.

'I've never seen it look so beautiful,' said Rohan. 'Perhaps now at last I can see why Decima loved it so much.'

The blank windows stared at them unseeingly. As they drew nearer they saw the garden was more wild and untended than ever and that the gamekeeper's little croft was already falling into ruins.

They reached the jetty. Rohan manoeuvred the boat into position and jumped ashore to fasten the painter to the bollard.

'The boards of the jetty aren't too secure,' he warned her. 'Careful how you go.'

'Thanks.' She scrambled ashore and stood still for a moment. The sea-breeze fanned her cheek; a gull screamed above her. Everywhere was very still.

'I'm going up to the house,' said Rohan. 'You needn't come if you don't want to, but I'm curious as to what's happened and what it looks like now.'

She was glad he gave her the chance to refuse. 'I'll stay here.' she said. 'I don't particularly want to go back.'

'Okay. I won't be long.'

She watched him move quickly up the path to the house. When he reached the front door he discovered it was locked and she saw him go round to the back and disappear from sight.

She waited some time in the sunshine, and then slowly the curiosity began to seep through her until she wished she had gone with him. After dreading the return to Ruthven so violently, it now seemed that the reality of return was not nearly as disturbing as she had feared it might be, and in the relief of realizing this she wanted to go into the house and try to blunt the edge of her worst memories by revisiting the scenes under different circumstances.

Presently she left the deck and stepped ashore on to the creaking jetty again. It took her about five minutes to reach the house. Rohan, she discovered, had climbed in through the kitchen window which might or might not have been broken before his arrival. As she was wearing slacks it was easy enough for her to clamber in after him, and soon she was walking through the huge deserted rooms and making her way into the massive emptiness of the great hall.

'Rohan?' she called uncertainly as she reached the foot of the stairs, but there was no reply.

Presently she mounted the staircase and then paused to listen. It was very quiet, very still. The sunshine streamed through the long windows of the hall, but the house was eerie in its deserted emptiness and Rachel was conscious of the smell of damp and decay.

She moved down the corridor and paused for a time outside the door of Decima's room, but suddenly her courage ebbed and she hadn't enough left to turn the handle and walk in. She went back down the passage to the head of the stairs and all at once it seemed to her as if she were re-enacting her movements on the night of the murders and she had just stopped outside Decima's door to ask her if she were all right. She reached the landing and paused to look down into the hall.

She could see the scene then as if it were yesterday, the long banquet table, the red candles snuffed and gutted, the remains of the dinner still strewn over the white tablecloth, the twin silver epergnes, the drooping flowers. Around the hall were the lamps, still burning, and the red embers in the two fire-places. George, the St Bernard, had been asleep before the hearth. Or had he? No. that had been earlier. When she had returned to the hall to find Charles, George had been asleep outside the door of the small drawing-room. She could remember wondering why he had chosen to lie in that draughty corner when both fires were still glowing in the grates.

As she began to descend the stairs it suddenly occurred to her to wonder again why the dog had been lying there. If Daniel had been in the drawing-room, then it would have explained the dog's presence, for George had followed Daniel everywhere, but Daniel had been upstairs talking to Decima in her room.

Or had he?

She stopped dead.

She was recalling the scene in the library when she had found Charles. There had been the closing of a door far away, the sound of footsteps crossing the hall and then Daniel had entered the room just after she had managed to hide behind the curtains. He had come from across the hall, from the drawing-room. She would never have heard the door of Decima's room close. It had been the door of the drawing-room where the dog was waiting for him.

Daniel hadn't been in Decima's room at all.

Then who had been with her as Rachel passed the door? Rebccca? But it had been a man's low murmur she had heard. Not Daniel. And not Charles, who was already dead. That left Rohan. Rohan had been with Decima just before she died.

But Rohan had been blind drunk. She had had to put him to bed.

Or had he been shamming? She had thought at the time that for two persons accustomed to liquor they had managed to get surprisingly drunk. Supposing it had all been an act, a plan to set the stage – for what?

For Charles' murder . . .

Rebecca had been framed. Rohan, thanks to Rachel's testimony, would be found to be much too drunk to commit a crime. And Decima . . . Daniel had carried Decima upstairs to her room. He would also testify that she had been too drunk to commit murder. But Daniel hadn't stayed in Decima's room because when Rachel reached the hall on her way to find Charles, George was already outside the drawing-room door waiting for Daniel to come out. And Decima, Rachel knew, had at that time been alive and well.

Daniel hadn't killed Decima. Rebecca? No, because the voice talking to Decima had belonged to a man. And Charles was already dead.

Rohan had killed Decima. And either he or Decima had first killed Charles.

Rohan was a murderer was all she was conscious of thinking, her frightened thoughts repeating themselves over and over again in a paralysis of horror. *Rohan was a murderer*.

And then the full impact of the situation struck her and she was so unnerved that she could neither move nor breathe.

Rohan was a murderer and she was alone with him at Ruthven.

CHAPTER TWO

I

Daniel rose early, had hired a car by eight-thirty and by nine o'clock had left Inverness behind and was driving west over the Highlands to Kyle of Lochalsh. It was raining. Clouds obscured the mountains, and mist trailed over the vast expanses of sodden moors. There were few other cars on the road. The rain slewed remorselessly on to the windscreen to make driving difficult, and as he drove on over that storm-torn landscape it seemed to him that the five hot steamy years in Accra had been a dream and that he had never left this beautiful appalling remoteness with its rains and mists and pale shrouded northern light.

This is real Scotland, he thought. Glasgow is for the businessmen; Edinburgh is for the tourists. But up here north of the Highland Line is the Scotland which is for no one, least of all for intruders, the Scotland which made even the Romans turn back unnerved in retreat. No wonder they believed it was the very edge of the world, the remotest corner of land known to man. The mountains are crowded together as if waiting to entomb all trespassers in the valleys, and the moors rise up from the road like the sides of a grave.

The heavy rain continued for some time. He was just wondering if there was any possibility at all of a break in the weather, when the road surmounted a pass and suddenly the clouds lifted from the mountain slopes, the rain lessened, and the sky seemed brighter. Within twenty minutes the highest of the inland mountains were behind him and he had travelled into a different world; the sun shone, the sky was blue and as he descended from the hills to Kyle of Lochalsh he could see that the horizon of the Atlantic was hazy with the promise of good weather.

He drove into the town.

Outside the small inn where he and Charles had often stopped for a beer after a shopping expedition, he parked the car and went inside. The landlord's wife was industriously sweeping out the bar with a long broom.

'Good morning,' she began brightly, and then stopped in stupefaction as she recognized him.

'Good morning,' he said, and waited for her to give him the information he wanted.

'Well!' she said amazed. 'Well!' And when he was silent, she added: 'It *is* Mr Carey, isn't it?'

'It is. You've got a good memory, Mrs MacCleod.'

She was pleased that he remembered her name. 'Well, now,' she said sympathetically. 'What a shame! You've just missed them – they were staying down the road at the Stuart Arms. My husband was over there talking to Ian Black, the landlord, when they arrived last night, and he said—'

'They've already gone?'

'Hired a boat this morning from Duncan Robertson – I saw them walk along the quay just a little while ago—'

'How long ago?'

She looked vaguely surprised by the abruptness of his questions. 'Why, two or three hours ago, perhaps. I'd just lit the fire in the kitchen and then I came in here to listen to the weather forecast on the wireless, and lo and behold, who should I see when I looked out of the window but Mr Quist and the young lady walking past to the quay . . . How long will you all be staying here, Mr Carey? Such a surprise to see you again. I said to my husband—'

'Not long,' said Daniel. 'Thank you, Mrs MacCleod.' And before the woman could even draw breath to say goodbye he was moving swiftly out of the house and down to the quayside and the harbour.

II

Rachel's first thought was to find the gun. Blindly, almost without thinking, she went out of the hall and back through the kitchens again to the broken window. As if in a nightmare her movements seemed curiously slow and clumsy; the window through which she had climbed with such ease earlier now seemed a difficult and dangerous obstacle in her path, and she cut her hand slightly on a piece of broken glass as she scrambled over the sill.

I must get back to the boat, she thought. *I must find that gun.*

There was no other thought in her mind at all. Her eyes saw the brilliant sparkle of the sun on the sea and clear sky, but they made no impression on her. She ran down towards the jetty, pushing her way through the overgrown garden, and soon she was gasping for breath and her heart was pounding in her lungs.

I must get to the boat, said the voice in her mind over and over again. *I must find the gun.*

She went on running. It seemed a long way to the jetty, and again she was reminded of some hideous nightmare in which one ran and ran yet never reached one's destination. Brambles tore at her slacks; giant bushes and unwieldy shrubs leered in her face and then suddenly she was out of the garden and running along the path down to the jetty.

I must get to the boat, she kept thinking. *I have to find that gun.*

Her foot stumbled against a rock; she nearly fell, and then at last she reached the rotting boards of the jetty and scrambled aboard the boat. She went to the wheelhouse. No gun. He must have left it below. She was beside the hatch suddenly, almost falling down the gangway to the lower deck. She could picture the gun lying on the top of Rohan's suitcase, and the suitcase was tossed across one of the bunks. . . .

She flung open the cabin door with a gasp of relief and then felt the gasp freeze in her throat.

'Hullo,' said Rohan. 'I thought I'd lost you. Where did you go?'

Instinct made her brain miraculously clear; her reactions were suddenly as sharp as a razor-edge.

'I went to the house and couldn't find you.' She made no effort to hide the fact that she had been running, and sank down on the bunk opposite him to regain her breath. 'Then suddenly I had an awful panic and saw ghosts in every corner. I ran all the way back here.'

'So it seems!' He smiled at her reassuringly. He had the gun in his hands and was checking to see that it was loaded correctly. He looked calm and untroubled, and the very familiarity of his expression and attitude gave Rachel a strange confidence. This was the Rohan she had known all her life, her friend of nearly all her life, the man whom she knew better than anyone else.

Rohan wouldn't harm her.

He stood up. 'Daniel won't be here for a while yet,' he said, tucking the gun into his belt. 'Let's take some of the food we bought in Kyle and walk along the beach away from the house. I don't want to sit on deck and look at Ruthven. I'm not surprised you felt panic-stricken when you went inside! I felt much the same myself.'

'Where were you?' she said. 'I couldn't find you anywhere.'

He moved to the door. 'I went to Decima's room,' he said abruptly, and for a moment she thought he wasn't going to add any more. Then: 'I shouldn't have gone. It was horrible.'

He went up on deck and she followed him.

'Why did you go?' she said.

'I don't know,' he said, and his eyes as he turned to look at her were dark and blank. 'I don't know. It was as if she were up there waiting for me, challenging me to come back.' He stepped on to the jetty, and then hesitated. 'We forgot the food.'

'We can always come back,' she said, 'and I'm not hungry.'

'All right.' He walked down the jetty and led the way out to the beach.

The sun was warm; the surf roared in their ears; beneath their feet the sand was firm and smooth. They walked for a long time in silence, and beside them towered the cliffs with the gaping caves and litter of black rocks embedded in the white sand. The tide was still going out. Rohan seemed engrossed in his private thoughts, and Rachel, her initial panic overcome, felt ice-cool and alert. It was not until they rounded the promontory that she was aware of the ache of tension in her body and the fear crawling up and down her spine.

'We're at the quicksands.' Her voice was harsh and abrupt.

'So we are,' said Rohan. He stood still, gazing out over the miles of white beach ahead shining deceptively in the bright light. 'Cluny Sands. Just lying there peaceful in the sun. Waiting.' He turned to face her. 'It's odd,' he said. 'But I feel so strongly as if everything here was waiting The house was waiting, the shore was waiting and now these sands are waiting too.'

Rachel turned aside sharply. 'That's melodramatic, Rohan, and you know it. Don't be absurd.'

'But don't you feel it?' he said. 'Don't you? Don't you feel that everything is poised and waiting?'

'I could imagine all kinds of things if I wanted to,' she heard herself answer tersely. 'If one stays in these surroundings long enough one could imagine anything. It's that kind of place.'

She hoped he couldn't hear the thumping of her heart, nor see the trembling of her clenched hands.

'Let's sit down,' he said. 'Let's sit down for a while.'

'Why?'

'Why?' he said. 'Why, to wait for Daniel, of course. We're waiting too now, just like everything else. Everything's waiting for Daniel.'

III

Daniel took the boat far out to sea before heading north to Ruthven. He had no wish to be blatantly visible from the beach and he was already trying to decide where to land. If he went to the jetty he would immediately announce his arrival. Perhaps if he were to try and anchor near the beach between Ruthven and Cluny Sands he would run less risk of Rohan seeing him immediately. It might be worth trying, although he was un-accustomed to boats after five years away from them, and did not want to risk running aground in shallow waters.

The boat sped on over the calm sea and left a wake trailing in the dark blue water. The air was full of warmth and peace, and the gulls soared aloft on the soft breeze, their wings white arcs against the sky.

He lit a cigarette.

He was thinking of Rachel again, visualizing her with Quist, unknowing and unsuspecting, being carried deeper and deeper into dangerous waters, manoeuvred into a position from which she could not escape. He was conscious of how his attitude towards her had changed. He had left Accra to protect his sister, to warn Rachel to say nothing to Quist about the false verdict at the inquest, and had instead discovered that his sister was entirely innocent. She had insisted her innocence and he had believed her; her protests were too genuine to be disbelieved. And then, even before he had time to feel ashamed of his suspicions, he had realized the extreme danger of Rachel's position. If Rachel once revealed the full extent of her knowledge to Quist she would always be a potential source of danger to him. The number of suspects was so small; she had no doubt left Ruthven believing Rebecca to be guilty, probably even suspecting Daniel himself to be in some way involved, but if she once thought them innocent there was only Rohan Quist left to suspect . . .

And Quist was a murderer who had killed before and would kill again. Daniel could remember thinking how ironic it was that Decima, who had been without passion herself, should in the end have been the victim of a *crime passionel*.

And now Rachel was alone with Quist at Ruthven. Perhaps by this time she had guessed the truth. If she were to hint for one moment to Quist that she suspected him . . .

Daniel threw away his cigarette.

There was no time to lose.

IV

She was almost sure that Rohan was asleep. He was lying face downwards on the sands, his head pillowed in his forearms, his breathing quiet and even. The gun, which he had taken out of his belt for greater comfort, lay peacefully beside him, its barrel glinting in the sunlight.

She picked it up.

Rohan didn't stir.

How did one remove the bullets from guns? If she could somehow take out the bullets, then Daniel would be safe, and she could return the gun to Rohan so that he would never know she had tampered with it.

She stood up very slowly, gun in hand. The tide had turned, she noticed; the waves were creeping back over the sands and the thunder of the surf seemed more powerful in her ears. She moved nearer the cliffs, and then all of a sudden she was amongst the rocks and Rohan could no longer see her.

She looked down at the gun in her hands and examined it.

It was unnerving not to be able to see Rohan, not to know whether he was still asleep. In a sudden moment of panic she moved back to the shore, but he was still sleeping, his position unchanged, and she felt her body relax slightly in relief.

It was then that she heard the suck of the undertow as the tide crept in over the quicksands.

Withdrawing behind a rock again she struggled with the gun, and at last, just as she was giving up hope, the metal broke open and the bullets spilled into her hands.

She went back to Rohan, stopped just long enough to put the gun down beside him and then went as close as she dared to the sands.

The bullets were soon gone. She had thrown them into the sands in the path of the incoming tide and they only took a few seconds to vanish from sight. She was just wiping the sweat from her forehead and pushing back her hair when his voice said softly from behind her: 'Why the hell did you do that?' and whirling round she found herself face to face with him and her back to Cluny Sands.

V

'So you know,' he said. 'I wondered if you did.'

He stood watching her, his blue shirt brilliant against the background of sand and rock, his fair hair shining in the sun, his eyes dark, opaque, expressionless. After a moment he said: 'How did you know?'

And she said: 'I realized just now in the hall that Daniel hadn't been with Decima just before she died. The scene jogged my memory and I realized then that Daniel had been downstairs in the drawing-room when I had gone to the library to find Charles. He wasn't in Decima's room, and yet I'd heard a man's voice there. And then I knew that you had pretended to be drunk earlier and that, after I'd left you, you'd slipped out to the library.'

'I went to Decima's room first to get Rebecca's diary and the knife.' He half-turned so that he faced the sea, and she saw that his hands were clenched as he thrust them into his pockets. Presently he said: 'It's hard for me to explain my feelings for Decima. How can a woman ever understand? I was infatuated with her. She was an obsession with me. For a long time after she married Charles I tried to pretend that there was no infatuation and no obsession, but you can't pretend for ever that black is white and white is black. And every time I went back to Ruthven my hatred for Charles grew and the pretence of not caring for Decima grew harder.

'Do you remember how I used to admire Charles – almost hero-worshipped him, when we were young? My distinguished cousin! My respected, esteemed, learned cousin who taught at Oxford and was one of the great scholars of his day! Charles was everything I knew I could never be. No wonder I admired him so much. And then gradually the beginnings of the long disillusionment set in, and I saw everything I had believed in was a myth, a self-deception. Charles was a brilliant scholar, but he was weak, opinionated, vain and pompous. And worst of all, he had won Decima, the greatest prize for any man to win, and then he had estranged and antagonized her so that she wanted only to be rid of him. Can you imagine how I felt? Can't you see? The more I allowed myself to admit my obsession for Decima the more I hated Charles, and all the while I had to conceal my feelings, to pretend and pretend and pretend . . . Something happens to a man when all the most violent passions are twisted together within him and suppressed again and again. You live in an unreal world and only your thoughts and wishes are reality. I wished Charles dead and that Decima were mine – that was my reality. I lived with that wish for a long time until it was more real to me than anything else in the world. It was a reality even before I began my last visit to Ruthven . . .

'I remember very well the first time I saw Daniel Carey. I had just arrived at Kyle of Lochalsh and was drinking beer in the pub overlooking the harbour when I saw Charles' boat draw up to the quay. Daniel was with Decima. I knew as soon as I saw him that nothing would ever be the same again and, even as I watched them laughing together while they walked down the quay, I was convinced that she loved him.'

The tide crept nearer; a huge wave broke and rushed greedily towards them as it ate into virgin sand.

'And then you came,' he said. 'And miraculously, almost unbelievably, Daniel seemed to tire of Decima and turn to you. It was then, and not till then, that Decima turned to me and it seemed at last that I was going to get everything I'd ever wanted.

'I suppose Decima guessed from the beginning how I felt for her. You remember she told you – to confuse you – that Charles was glad you'd come to Ruthven because it would divert her attention from me, and that Charles suspected us of having an affair? That was untrue, for Charles knew nothing about how I felt, but I got a bad shock when you repeated the story to me! I then realized that Decima had merely told you that to throw you off the scent and conceal from you her involvement with Daniel. At that time, of course, there was nothing between us, but I think she sensed my feelings nonetheless. Women have an instinct for divining how a man cares, I think, no matter how much he may lie and pretend to the contrary out of pride, and so when she realized at last that she could no longer rely on Daniel she came at once to me for help.

'It was the day of the dinner-party. She said she wanted the opportunity to talk to me alone, so we took the boat and went out to sea, intending just to cruise around in open waters for a while, but then as you know a storm blew up and we had to head for Kyle for shelter. We spent quite a long time at sea before we had to seek shelter. She let me do exactly as I wished. Later, when we were in Kyle waiting for the storm to die, she told me she would marry me if she were free but that Charles had now quite made up his mind not to divorce her, and it seemed that she was tied to him indefinitely.

'We were drinking by that time. Alcohol seemed to clarify the situation and make everything so obvious.

' "I would kill Charles," she said, "but I'd be too afraid, too frightened . . . And how could I kill him? I haven't the strength or the knowledge." She seemed so powerless, so vulnerable, so young . . .

'I said: "I'd kill him for you, if I could."

'I should have guessed then what was happening, because she had the whole scheme ready and planned – she must have worked it out as soon as she had discarded her plans for using Daniel the day before, and she already had Rebecca's knife and diary hidden in readiness. I should have realized that she was only using me, just as she had tried to use Daniel, but I was long past sane, sensible reasoning, far beyond all sanity and logic.

' "It would be so easy," she said. "Can't you see? Every-thing is already set perfectly. Rebecca has the ideal motive for murdering Charles. We can use her knife to kill him and set the scene to make it look as if she killed him in a fit of rage – he has, after all, just ended their affair against her will. I saw her this morning weeping and red-eyed, and Charles had told me by that time that he was sending the Careys away. Rebecca is the perfect scapegoat – but we must take care no suspicion falls on us. We'll go back tonight at the end of the dinner-party and pretend to be drunk out of our minds. The dinner-party will collapse in chaos, and someone will see us to our rooms. As soon as you're sure the coast's clear, you can come back to my room, and I'll give you the dagger and Rebecca's diary which I stole from her earlier. Then after it's done you can go back to your room and no one will ever know that we weren't really drunk at all, and after it's all over we can go away together." '

A gull wheeled and soared high over the sea. Behind them the tide was still sucking over the quicksands but they no longer heard it.

'So it wasn't Decima who killed Charles,' Rachel heard herself say. 'It was you.'

'Yes,' he said. 'I killed him. After you'd led me to bed I waited and then went to Decima's room. Daniel carried her upstairs a few minutes later and I hid in the cupboard till he'd gone. Decima asked him where Charles was and he said that Charles had gone to the library.

'I took the knife and the diary and went down the back stairs to the kitchen. Mrs Willie had gone back to her croft so there was no one about, and when I reached the hall I saw that too was empty – apart from the dog sleeping outside the drawing-room door.

'I went to the library. Charles was just sitting with his head in his hands. He didn't even see the dagger until I was much too close for him to avoid it, and he died almost at once. No one saw me leave the library afterwards. I retraced my steps up the back stairs and went to Decima's room to tell her that all was well, and that was when you passed by in the corridor and heard us talking.

'It was after you'd gone that my whole world collapsed. I started to talk to Decima of when we would go away together, but she wasn't interested. I tried to kiss her, but she was lifeless, cold as a statue, remoter from me than she'd ever been.

' "What's the matter?" I said frantically. "What have I done?" And then suddenly, hideously, I saw the truth.

'She cared for me no more than she cared for anyone else. She was completely egocentric, a narcissus in love with herself, withdrawn from other beings and beyond their reach in her own private world. Charles was an obstacle in her path so he had to be removed. How could she remove him without getting hurt herself? Why, get someone else to murder him for her! Why not? Men were always falling over themselves to do as she wished. At first she thought Daniel would probably be just like all the others. He would do as well as anyone. But first of all she must plan very carefully so that no suspicion could possibly fall on her.

'She was aware that Charles was having an affair with Rebecca, but she didn't plan then, as she did later, to frame Rebecca for Charles' murder. She had planned a scheme long before she knew about Charles and Rebecca, and it was this scheme which she intended to put into operation. She was to act the part of the terrified young wife in fear of her husband but much too nervous and weak to attempt to remove him. Then, after Charles was dead, she could sob on the Chief Detective-Inspector's shoulder and confess that Daniel Carey had been so in love with her that he had killed Charles to prevent her suffering any further and to remove her from all danger.

'But first of all she had to create the impression of the terrified young wife, and to do that she needed an audience.

'So she invited you to Ruthven and spun you the story about Charles wanting to kill her. You were to be her audience, the witness who would later back up her story to the police. That was why you were invited to Ruthven.

'And then everything went wrong with that scheme and got out of hand so that she was forced to reshape her plans. You fell in love with Daniel and she knew she could never trust you to give evidence for her against him. At the same time she realized that Daniel wasn't so infatuated with her that he would kill for her. In fact, he wasn't infatuated at all.

'So she used me. She tore down the façade I had presented to everyone since her marriage and destroyed all my defences and then gathered together all my love and hate and twisted them into her own distorted pattern. And it wasn't until afterwards in her room that I realized what she had done.

'I have no memory after that. I remember staring at her as I recognized the truth and then nothing at all except isolated things – pulling open the window, the rush of cold air, my hand on her mouth as she tried to scream. I flung her from me as if I would smash every ounce of bone and blood in her evil rotten body, and after that there was just a dreadful blankness until I reached my room again and locked the door against the nightmare of what had happened . . . I've been trying to keep my mind locked against it ever since. The last five years have been one long struggle to shut out all the dreadful memories and submerge myself in something new and far away in another world, but there are some things you can't shut out no matter how much you want to, and when I came back here today and went to her room I knew I would never get rid of them, never, no matter how long I lived and no matter where I went.'

The surf broke down the beach and sped swiftly across the sands to their feet. It touched Rohan's shoes but he seemed not to notice for he made no effort to step back.

'I'm glad I've told you,' he said after a while. 'I've wanted to tell you for a long time. Perhaps that's why I asked you to marry me. I'd have been safe if we were married, because a wife can't give evidence against her husband.'

He was still looking out to sea, and suddenly she saw him stiffen. 'There's a boat out there,' he said, pointing behind her over her shoulder. 'A small boat a long way out – can you see it?'

Rachel spun round.

At the same moment a huge wave broke and streaked up to her, knocking her off her balance, and even as she stumbled backwards before falling, she heard the roar of the undertow and the greedy sucking of the quicksands beneath her feet.

VI

Daniel saw the blue of Rohan's shirt from out at sea, and immediately altered his course to head inland. As he drew closer he strained his eyes to see what was happening on the beach but beyond the fact that Quist and Rachel were by the water's edge and Rachel appeared to be on her knees he had no idea what they were doing.

And then Quist started to run. Almost at the same moment Daniel realized that Rachel, who was still motionless, was on the edge of Cluny Sands.

Pulling out the throttle he revved the engine into a higher speed and headed straight for the beach.

VII

Rohan saw the boat coming and stopped in his tracks. It came on without faltering and then, just as he thought it must surely come aground, the engines were cut and Daniel, emerging from the wheelhouse, stooped to the deck to pick up the anchor and fling it overboard. Then he stooped again and this time when he straightened his back he had a coil of rope in his hands.

Rohan thought for a moment, his brain suddenly cool, sharp

168

and detached. If he were lucky he could easily deal with Daniel, who would be much too preoccupied with the rescue to notice Rohan's movements. And Rachel . . . Rachel was stuck in the quicksand. He could always say afterwards that he had been unable to reach her. Two victims for the quicksands. He could almost see the newspaper headlines. Dual tragedy on remote Scottish coast, heroism of lone survivor . . .

He stood his ground, waiting.

On the boat Daniel had slung the rope over his shoulder and was lowering himself into the shallows. As he moved swiftly through the water to the shore he made no attempt to speak and Rohan found his silence curiously unnerving.

'I was going back to the house,' he heard himself say rapidly as Daniel came abreast of him. 'There's a ladder there. I thought if I could crawl along the ladder I could reach her. I wasn't running away.'

Daniel pushed past him without a word, and broke into a run.

'Daniel—' Rohan stared after him blankly for a moment, and then pulling himself together he ran back along the beach to where Rachel had left his empty gun.

VIII

'Wait,' said Daniel to Rachel. 'Don't move. The more you struggle the farther in you'll sink.' He was uncoiling the rope, as he spoke, his fingers working to tie the last yard into a noose.

'Rohan was going to get a ladder,' she said, and her voice was shaking in spite of all her efforts to keep calm. 'He said there was a ladder in the gardening shed.'

'He told me.' The knot was tied, the rope firm beneath his fingers. 'Now listen,' he said. 'Listen. I'm going to throw this to you. Slip the noose around you body and hold onto the rest of the rope as hard as you can. Can you manage that?'

'Yes.'

Another wave broke. She felt the sands sucking at her legs, pulling them sickeningly downwards, and suddenly the horror of it all was in every part of her and she hardly knew how to stifle her screams.

'Ready?'

'Yes.'

And even as he threw the rope towards her she saw Rohan moving up behind with the butt of the gun glinting in his hand.

'Daniel—'

But he was much too quick for her to complete the sentence. As soon as he saw her expression change he had whirled round, dropping the rope on the sands, and had caught Rohan's upraised arm before the blow could fall.

They struggled. The tide swirled forward over their naked feet, and suddenly Rachel's mind was a mere camera incapable of any emotional reaction as it recorded the scene like a strip of film before her eyes.

The gun spun out of Rohan's hand into the quicksands and was gone a second later. Rohan took a step backwards. Then another. And as his feet began to sink he lurched forward towards firmer ground and the blow from Daniel's fist caught him so cleanly on the jaw that unconsciousness must have come immediately. He keeled backwards, his feet staggering from the weight of the blow, and even as Rachel opened her mouth to scream, he fell full length into the quicksands and the waves surged forward greedily over his body.

The world spun dizzily. She would have fallen, but the sand was up to her waist so that falling was impossible, and then just as she hovered on the brink of consciousness she felt the rope tighten round her body and Daniel's voice ringing in her ears.

'Hold the rope!' he was shouting. 'Pull as hard as you've ever pulled in your life! Pull, for God's sake!'

The rope was rough and seared her palms. Another wave disturbed the sands and suddenly her hips were free. She clung on, trying to move her feet, and again another wave helped her and shifted the sand. She pulled until she felt she would pull no longer, and suddenly her ankles were free and she was half-skidding, half-floating along the shifting sands.

She felt tears blur her eyes, her limbs lock in a paralysis of exhaustion, and then his hand was reaching for hers, pulling her back out of the long nightmare which had begun five years ago to the peace of another saner world beyond.

Three days later, Rebecca Carey received a letter from her brother.

'It seems as if I shall be delayed in Scotland for longer than I thought,' he had written. 'The whole story is much too complicated to put in a letter so I shall have to explain the situation more fully when I see you. However to put it as briefly as possible, I reached Ruthven to find Rachel trapped on Cluny Sands by a rising tide, and managed to pull her to safety by a rope from the boat I'd hired. Quist wasn't so lucky. I'm sorry to tell you this, as I know you were seeing a great deal of him recently, but in trying to rescue Rachel he himself was trapped and died despite our efforts to reach him. I hope you won't be too upset by this. Perhaps when you feel ready to do so you could telephone his family, whom the authorities have already notified, and say that he died trying to save Rachel's life.

'Now perhaps you can guess one of the reasons for the delay, if not the other. When we got back to Kyle of Lochalsh we told the police what had happened and they have asked us to stay for the inquest, which will be held on the day you receive this letter. Then, after the inquest is closed and the matter ended, I shall be driving Rachel back to Inverness (where I hired a car) and travelling from there by train to Edinburgh where we shall be staying for a further seventeen days. You will, of course, be utterly astonished to know that I shall be staying with Rachel in Edinburgh for an apparently arbitrary choice of seventeen days, so I had better explain that one is permitted to be married in Scotland if one has been resident in that country for three weeks. We have so far been resident four days so that leaves seventeen days unaccounted for.

'I do realize that this news will be something of a surprise to you, but I know you're far too intelligent not to realize how fine a person Rachel is and how fortunate I am to be able to marry her. Let me know when you'll be arriving for the wedding, won't you? We'll be staying at the North Briton Hotel near Princes Street, and you can contact us there.

'Rachel asks rather shyly (I wonder why?) to be remembered to you. I send my love as always, of course, and look forward to seeing you again as soon as possible.

'Your brother,
Daniel.'

Susan Howatch
Cashelmara £2.50

A glorious, full-blooded novel which centres on Cashelmara, a coldly
beautiful Georgian house in Galway, ancestral home of Edward de Salis.
The fast-moving plot follows the turbulent fortunes of an aristocratic
Victorian family through half a century of furious encounters, ill-advised
liaisons and bitter-sweet interludes of love.

'Another blockbluster from Susan Howatch' SUNDAY TIMES

Penmarric £1.95

'I was ten years old when I first saw the inheritance and twenty years
older when I saw Janna Roslyn, but my reaction to both was identical,
I wanted them.' The inheritance is Penmarric, a huge, gaunt house in
Cornwall belonging to the tempestuous, hot-blooded Castallacks;
Janna Roslyn is a beautiful village girl who becomes mistress of Laurence
Castallack, wife to his son . . .

'A fascinating saga . . . has all the right dramatic and romantic ingredients'
WOMAN'S JOURNAL

The Devil on Lammas Night £1.25

When Tristan Poole moved to a remote Welsh village, was it to form
a nudist group? Or was it, as Nicola Morrison suspected, for something
much more sinister? What was the hypnotic effect Tristan had on her
mother? What was the cause of the sudden accident and deaths at
Colwyn? And what was Tristan planning for Nicola? As Lammas night
approaches, the true, supernaturally evil nature of the group is revealed
and Nicola is drawn into deadly danger . . .

The Rich are Different £1.95

A great fortune and the struggle to control a worldwide business
empire; an ambitious and beautiful woman who is one of the most
provocative heroines in fiction; a love that spans ecstasy and anguish
and a story that reaches from the quiet Norfolk countryside across the
ocean to the New York of the Roaring Twenties.

'Love, hate, death, murder and a hell of a lot of passion'
DAILY MIRROR

Barbara Michaels
The Sea King's Daughter 75p

The latest spellbinder from the author of *Greygallows*, the story is set on
the Greek island of Thera, where Sandy Bishop's father, an archaeologist,
is searching for traces of the lost civilization of Atlantis.
Frightening things begin to happen, and Sandy feels some force is
keeping her there . . . A terrifying power from the distant past and the
real dangers of the present close in a trap . . .

House of Many Shadows 70p

Meg's mind still played tricks on her after her head injuries from the
accident had healed. When she tried a change of scene by moving to the
old house cousin Sylvia had inherited, the hallucinations would not go
away. The shadows and presences of horror came more often in the
silent rooms . . .

'A heady blend of romance, murder and the supernatural'
OXFORD TIMES

Greygallows 60p

Forced into marriage to Baron Clare, Lucy Cartwright, a young and
beautiful heiress is taken to Greygallows, his forbidding Yorkshire
estate, where she is kept a prisoner, subject to the caprices of her
husband, whose behaviour alternates between gallantry and brutality.
Terrified and bewildered, Lucy gradually discovers the terrible meaning
of the Curse of the Clares . . .

The Crying Child 60p

Mary listened for the dreadful keening sound that always came in the
still of the night. The desolate wail of a small child that was slowly
destroying her . . . Joanne, her sister, sought an answer to her secret
fears. Was Mary becoming dangerously unbalanced? Then Joanne heard
the voice herself . . .

Carola Salisbury
The Dolphin Summer 75p

Annabel Trewella came aboard the steam yacht *Dolphin* in October 1897 as companion to the delicate Melloney, bound for the North African coast in search of warmth and sunshine. But for Annabel the delights of the cruise were soon tinged with mystery and fear. Who was it who sobbed heartbroken in the night? Who had written the cryptic messages on the glass of her porthole? And why is the memory of her long dead half-sister linked to a terrible sin?

'Splendid' YORKSHIRE POST

Mallion's Pride 95p

Castle Mallion, the great house on the wild Cornish coast, held many secrets for Joanna Goodacre, transported there from Jamaica by Benedict Trevallion, Mallion's new master . . . Benedict makes Joanna his bride – but a bride in name only. She is threatened by Benedict's servants and tormented by Mayana, the half-caste who visits her husband in the dead of night: and, against her will, Joanna comes to suspect her husband of past murders . . .

Dark Inheritance 95p

The dying words of her father cast a shadow over the strange destiny of Susannah, alone and friendless in a dangerous world . . . As governess at Landeric, the Cornish home of the Dewaines, Susannah becomes aware of dark secrets and hidden enemies – and she meets Mark Dewaine, handsome young cavalryman. The tide of fortune then sweeps her to Venice and more intrigue . . . then back to England, and the London of Victoria's heyday.

The Winter Bride 75p

For Charity Carewe it began as a dream come true. Martin Revesby invited her to become his secretary at his great house on the Cornish cliffs . . . But a sinister presence seemed to pervade the house. Could the beast of Malmaynes have risen from the grave? A gothic drama of passion and terror . . .

'Builds to a climax as clever as it is unexpected'
SHEFFIELD MORNING TELEGRAPH

Jessica Stirling
The Spoiled Earth £1.75

A powerful and exciting love story set against the loyalties and
oppressions, catastrophes and ambitions, of a nineteenth-century
Scottish mining community. This haunting saga traces the joys and
despairs of Mirrin Stalker, radical firebrand and tantalising beauty, who
is unprepared for the directions which her passions take . . .

'Jessica Stirling has a brilliant future' CATHERINE COOKSON

The Hiring Fair £1.50

This magnificent sequel to *The Spoiled Earth* is set in the Scotland of the
bleak 1870s. With her father and two brothers dead in the Blacklaw
mine disaster, Mirrin Stalker, the restless firebrand of the Stalker family,
takes to the road. Through tinker camp and hiring fair she finally
emerges on the stage of the music-hall in its bright-lit heyday.

The Dark Pasture £1.25

Seventeen years have passed since the events described in *The Spoiled
Earth* and *The Hiring Fair*. Mirrin, the strength and pride of the Stalker
family, is living at Hazelrig Farm with her husband and four children.
Against a background of the bitterness of the striking miners, Neill
Stalker stands accused of the murder of a special constable. Only one
thing can save the young collier. Neill is the bastard son of Drew
Stalker, now a wealthy and famous Edinburgh QC . . .